Save Me

CONSUMED SERIES
BOOK 2

Tris Wynters

Tris Wynters Publishing

© 2024 Tris Wynters Publishing. All rights reserved.

This book is a work of fiction. Any names, characters, companies, organizations, places, events, locales, and incidents are either used in a fictitious manner or are fictional. Any resemblance to actual persons, living or dead, actual companies or organizations, or actual events is purely coincidental.

For rights and permissions, please contact:

triswyntersbooklover23@gmail.com

This book is for those who crave golden boys that turn morally gray in the name of love. May their enemies rest in pieces.

Enjoy,
XOXO Tris

Contents

Dedication ... iii
Playlist ... ix

Warning ... 1
Content/Trigger Warnings ... 3
   1 Vince ... 5
   2 Cory ... 9
   3 Nick ... 13
   4 Jenson ... 16
   5 Vince- One hour earlier ... 21
   6 Nick ... 26
   7 Jenson ... 32
   8 Annie ... 41
   9 Vince ... 46
   10 Annie ... 52
   11 Vince ... 57
   12 Annie ... 63
   13 Cory ... 76

14	Annie	81
15	Nick- One week later	90
16	Annie	95
17	Jenson	103
18	Cory	109
19	Annie	120
20	Vince	127
21	Cory	134
22	Annie	139
23	Jenson- One Hour Ago	146
24	Annie	157
25	Annie	161
26	Vince- Thirty Minutes Ago	169
27	Nick	177
28	Cory	181
29	Annie	187

A note from the author	189
Acknowledgements	191

Save Me

Playlist

(Playlists can also be found on YouTube Music)

1. **Lose Control-** Teddy Swims
2. **Don't Give Up On Me-** Andy Grammer
3. **Paralyzed-** NF
4. **Heathens (Metal Cover)-** Leo
5. **Tears Don't Fall-** Bullet For My Valentine
6. **Beautiful Crazy-**Luke Combs
7. **Paint The Town Red-** Doja Cat

Warning

The Consumed Series is a dark, contemporary romance with adult themes. The FMC has multiple love interests and will not have to choose between them.

While I would love for you to enjoy this book, please keep your own mental health a priority. This book is **not** like the first. It contains heavier trigger warnings and our MCs will do a lot of damage in the name of love.

Human trafficking is the primary focus in this book so it gets **dark.** Discussion and implications of rape are insinuated but a full scene is not on page.

This book will end with a cliffhanger, sorry, but there will be an HEA; eventually.

Please be aware of your own triggers and limitations. A detailed list can be found on the next page.

If you are being trafficked, or you think someone else is, don't hesitate; get help.

Content/Trigger Warnings

* RH/ Polyamory
* Bi-Awakening
* BDSM References
* Adult Language
* Stalking/Harassment
* Self-harm- Accidental and Past
* Rape (full scenes not on page)
* Forced Drug Use
* Forced Paralysis
* Water Torture
* Disassociation
* C-Sections (Past)
* Multiples Birth (Past)
* NICU (Past)
* Sexual Assault
* Anxiety and Panic Attacks
* Kidnapping
* Trafficking
* Gang Violence
* Stabbing/Cutting
* Shooting
* Blood
* Branding
* Starvation
* Degradation

If you have any questions about content or trigger warning, please reach out to triswyntersbooklover23@gmail.com.

1

Vince

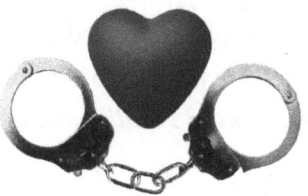

I have a bad case of the Mondays. I can't even tell what my actual problem is. I mean, there's no way it has anything to do with the sexy woman who poured out her soul to us; to my brothers and me. Who let herself be seen and vulnerable. Who let us in and then left her walls down, allowing us to truly see her, accept her, want her.

Her giggling at Jenson and I bickering about whether Dexter would really get away with those murders was so refreshing. Watching her snuggled up with Nick, *my* Nick, knowing they are both so jittery with touch, just about made my heart explode. He was so quick to accept her, and her touch that it shocked us all. Even initiating touch is hard for him. But not with her. He reacted so fast to her panic attack, and wrapped around her like a huge punk rock backpack. It would have been funny if it wasn't so heartbreaking. We all peeked in on them once, just to check on them. Once we saw that he clearly knew what she needed, we left them alone.

After she left, I asked Nick about what he did to her and why. I know he enjoys bondage, both doing and having done it to him. I know it's about comfort, trust, and peace for the submissive to be able to relinquish complete control. But I didn't know about how it can affect the nervous system and how it can help slow or even stop an anxiety attack. He said it doesn't work on everyone but he wanted to try anyway.

That's also when I found out about the anxiety attack she had at the gym. How they saw her try to beat the gym bag into submission before bursting into a fit of rage-fueled tears. Nick didn't second guess his gut then, either. He just ran to her; for her. *Damn I love that man. Have I told him recently? I really need to make a point to spend more time with him.*

I shake my head and try to concentrate on a tip we got about a possible Black Thorns storage location. It looks to be on the edge of town at a marina in Clear Lake. The entire area is a healthy mixture of residents and tourists making it ridiculously easy for these assholes to go unnoticed. All they need is a boat of any kind to blend in.

Clear Lake dumps right into Galveston Bay, which leads into the Gulf, making transporting illegal products far too easy. As a police officer in a city outside of Houston, I already know the trafficking statistics. I know Houston has the highest rate of human trafficking in the U.S. Not only because it's part of the "Texas Triangle", easily connected to Dallas and San Antonio, but also because we're close to two important borders. One being Mexico and the other being the Gulf. Both borders make trafficking victims easier to obtain and transport.

My stomach churns with unease and disgust. How the hell do you grow up to be a person who sells other people?? And some of the things I've heard and seen are straight from nightmares. *This is fucking sick. Worst case ever.*

So far, we know they transport weapons, drugs, women and children, and potentially organs. The last piece is still not solid but, given most of the bodies we connected had similar tox screen results and were missing various organs, it seems probable. I need to get with their local department first. See if they have any info on the area and make sure I don't get into trouble by snooping around.

I rub my hands over my face a few times, just letting the feeling soothe me. I hate this gang and its leaders. And I hate, more than anything, that Annie is wrapped up in this. *How does such a pure, sweet soul end up with a bastard like Lukas? Wait, nevermind, I know how.* People like him prey on others. He probably spotted her goodness and light a mile away. And what he put her through; Jesus! I know I don't know everything but what I do know is this woman is stronger than half the men I know. I am in awe of her ability to continue to smile, live, and fight for her kids to be shielded from his evil. *Fuck this, I need to get up for a bit.*

I grab my mug and wander over to the kitchen area. As I fill it, I take out my phone and text Annie. She should be just about done with her lessons for the morning.

> **Me-** Hey, Angel. Hope you enjoyed your day yesterday. We wanted to give you some space after Friday night.
> **Me-** Anyway, I'd love to have lunch with you sometime this week. Bringing the others is optional. <wink emoji>
> **Me-** Headed back into paperwork hell. Wish me luck. Have a great day, beautiful.

I can feel the goofy smile taking over my face. Just thinking about her and the time we have spent together lifts the weight from my shoulders. And I'd be lying if I said she isn't equal parts sweet and sexy. She doesn't even realize how we're all falling head over ass for her.

Shaking my head to clear images of her looking far too perfect in our home, I grab the coffee pot and fill up my mug. I take a huge gulp, relishing the burn as it slides down my throat. I let the scent of the arabica coffee, swirled with notes of vanilla and cinnamon, ground me. I can almost feel the caffeine pump through my veins, restoring my energy and renewing my focus. I take a deep breath, close my eyes and begin formulating my next steps. Walking back to my desk, I walk with renewed vigor. *I've got to find these assholes and put them all away.*

Just as I sit back at my desk, I hear, "Daniels, I need to speak with you." I recognize Captain's voice and snap my head up to look at him. He's walking from his office into an interrogation room. *Why the hell are we going in there? I don't have a suspect in.*

I stand and make my way through the office space. Right as Captain opens the door, he turns around to wait. But what I see on his face startles me to a stop. I tilt my head, scanning his face, his body, as if the words he is holding in will magically appear on his skin. He looks at me, his face trying to cling to an impassive mask but, I see it. Whatever he has to say, it's going to ruin my entire day.

2

Cory

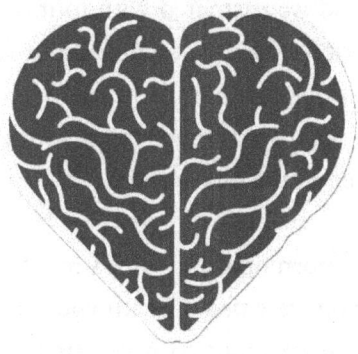

Saturday was emotionally draining. Pouring my heart out to Annie and releasing all of those feelings that have been building for this last month was *everything*. While it felt terrifying and exhilarating, nothing compared to how I felt while she tore open her chest and bared the darkest parts of her past. And then, oh and then, that amazing, strong, fierce woman still stood in front of us, sassier than ever, stepped into her armor, and gave us the choice: Take it or leave it. Take *her* or leave *her*.

I didn't have to analyze, didn't need a list, didn't go through every scenario possible. Nope, I already knew every scenario began and ended with her. I wanted her, all of her, and will gladly spend my life hoping for scraps of her attention.

I blink my eyes and remember that my meeting with the youth center is starting in ten minutes. I've apparently been staring at the paperwork for my sixth check but got distracted.

I reach for my phone, and smile at my screen saver. It's a picture I snuck of Annie curled up against Nick, a smile lighting up her whole face as she laughs at something Jense said. Now my own smile stretches across my face.

Jenson should be back with the coffee and pastries in a minute and then I really need to focus. We have so many great opportunities for these kiddos. And we partnered with four other local businesses to expand their options. I am so excited about this and I know the guys are, too. Of course, Annie's help and recommendations were invaluable. I know we shared some things with her but didn't get a chance to update her on the final bundle.

> **Me-** Good morning pretty girl! I missed you yesterday but I'm sure you were tied up with your kids. Just wanted you to know we're about to have our meeting with the youth center. We also have three of those places you looked into coming on board. I will call you after to update you. Hope you have a good day!

I stow my phone in my pocket before making my way to the front to wait for our visitors. Nick meets me in the hall. "Hey, Cor! You ready man?" He doesn't get outwardly excited about much but seeing his eyes light up and the smile stretching across his face is contagious. This deal means so much to him.

"You know it. I let Annie know it was about to start. I know she's been invested in this whole process, too." Nick's smile widens and he runs his hand over his hair. "Yeah, she really has. She offered more insight than we could have ever hoped for. And the science center? Genius!" I nod my head, grinning at the memory of her explaining all she found. The excitement on her face was breathtaking. It's a smile I look forward to seeing more; preferably multiple times per day.

"What up sexy bastards! Ready to make some kids happy?" Jenson comes strolling through the front door just as we get to the front desk. He's always been the clown of the group. Usually knowing when humor is needed, but not always. However we all know the man behind the carefully constructed mask he wears. He uses humor to hide the pain. Unfortunately for him, he can't always hide the nightmares that occasionally haunt him. They're the worst around his birthday and Christmas.

His dad overdosed when he was a kid. Jense found him in the bathroom, foam falling out of his mouth and eyes completely lifeless. After the funeral, Mommy dearest drank herself stupid and abusive men three miles long rotated through they're home. They paid Jense no mind, until they needed to take their aggressions out on someone smaller than them.

In high school, he found solace in the water, trying to out swim his nightmares, and day mares. He decided to go out for the swim team but knew his cuts and bruises would be questioned. To counter their curiosities, he spun tales of being a secret vigilante at night, fighting off people in alleyways and gas stations that were trying to be robbed. Then he claimed he and his cousins got rough wrestling around. But, we all knew; everyone knew.

The first day CPS showed up, his Mom's douchebag of the week beat him to the point of needing to be hospitalized. His mom never visited. Never showed. So, Jense made the decision to not go back. He was always at Vince's anyway. His dad had always told Jense he was welcome to live with them, that he was already like family. But

Jense never took him up on the offer until he was in that bed, alone and broken.

Shaking my head, I clear out the mental images left rattling in my brain and smile before saying, "Yup, let's do this! I can't wait to show them what we've put together. I let Annie know we would call her after." I take my phone out of my pocket, checking to see if she had responded. I bat away the disappointment when I don't have a notification. *She's busy. I know this. She isn't* my *mother. I* won't *let my past dictate our future.*

I take a deep breath to recenter myself. "All right, Jense, you stay here and wait for our guests. Nick and I will go make sure the room is set up." I grab the pastries and Nick grabs the coffee cart and pushes it down the hallway. I follow behind him, my excitement for this meeting building with every step.

3

Nick

I park the coffee cart and set out the creamers and other junk people may need. I am so damn excited I can hardly keep still. I barely got a wink of sleep last night, going over every detail in my head. It's been the same since I decided to get up this morning. I was so restless that at 4:00am, I hopped out of bed and went for an early run; then came here. I strolled right into this room and reviewed our slide deck repeatedly. I need to make sure every page is perfect. Each slide has a different program we want to offer along with all the data they, and we, need to make a decision. I make sure that every slide is clear, easy to understand, and the bullet points are direct.

I check the monitor, again, to make sure the screen is still sharing, open to our company logo. *It is. It has been for over an hour.* There's seriously nothing else that needs to be done except wait for our guests.

But, that doesn't keep me from busying myself with re-checking everything, again.

I hear Cory behind me, setting up the pastry platters across the table. I already know that when I turn around, each platter will be particularly placed on the table, with the perfect balance of each type of pastry to satisfy everyone. He likes everyone to have options and tries to prevent people from reaching over others. He's so damn meticulous. Always has been. He has spent his life making sure everything around him is *just* right. He had to learn far too young how to take care of himself, how to be responsible. He also learned that if he needed something, he had to get it himself. He had to *do* it all himself.

Now that we're all grown, some of the rigidity has decreased. He still utilizes those skills he was forced to learn but we try to make sure he sticks within his specific department. We don't want him killing himself trying to run the whole damn business himself; and he *would* try if we let him.

I turn, facing the room, before sitting in the chair closest to the computer. My knee starts bouncing, excitement thrumming through me as I wait for the meeting to start. I can't wait to hear what they say once we can share all of the plans. Hopefully, if they agree, we can get the programs up and running quickly. I know deep in my soul that this could help so many kids.

Hell, it would have helped us. We're lucky we found each other. We're all so jacked from our pasts, I'm not sure any one of us would have truly survived, truly lived, had we not been together.

Speaking of together... I slide my phone from my pocket and open the messaging app. I know Cory texted Annie but she's been on my mind since she walked out Saturday night. *Who am I kidding?* She's been on my mind since I saw her dancing at the club. My little Siren called out to me before she even knew who I was. Now, I feel the call to her no matter where she is. It's constantly there, tugging at me like we're two opposing magnets trying to find our way back to each other.

My thumb hovers over the typing bar. *Should I message? Would she want to hear from me? Is she really all in or has she backed away now that she's not with us, in our presence?*

Saturday was awful in more ways than ten but it was also amazing. Feeling her relax in my hold, watching her fight to be vulnerable with us, trusting us with her past; it was everything. But, she didn't stop there. Her inner fighter came out and it was so damn sexy. She may have left the decision up to us whether we still wanted to be with her, but what she doesn't understand is there was never a decision to be made. It was always going to be her with us. We are consumed by her and will do anything to cherish her, every day.

Me- Hey siren. Wanted to check in on you. Hope you got plenty of rest yesterday. We're about to start the presentation. I wish you were here. You really should be. So much of this is because of you and your brilliant brain. Anyway I know you're busy but I'll call you later. Hope something makes you smile today.

I stare at the screen for a moment, hoping to at least see the little three dots. But then, the door opens and Jense is waving his hand for the group to step inside. I slip my phone back in my pocket, stand up, and begin shaking their hands as Jenson offers introductions.

4

Jenson

It's showtime! I am so freaking excited I can feel myself vibrating as I make the introductions. Linda, the Youth Center's liaison, Gorge, the Martial Arts and Self-Defense instructor we found, Bridgette, the painting and art studio co-owner, Sean, the science center liaison, and Gabby, the co-owner of the nearby animal shelter and vet tech. All five of them are here with us to make a plan, a promise, to make a difference in the lives of the local youth. What. A. Feeling!

After introductions, I walk towards the front of the room, closest to the screen. "Well, ladies and gentlemen, please help yourself to some coffee from the cart to my right, and a delicious pastry from a bakery around the corner. Once you're all loaded up, please find a seat and we can get started." I give my best customer service smile, swipe a pastry onto a napkin, and take a seat across the table from Cory.

Cory spends the next hour going through the programs; days, times, everything. Everyone is equal parts excited and impressed that we could pull this together so quickly. But, now, I get to tell Linda the best part. I clear my throat and stand at the front of the room. "Well, Ms. Linda, what do you think?"

The little wisp of a woman with brown eyes and brown locks striped with purple streaks, turns her attention to me. Her eyes glisten with unshed tears and her smile is so wide her cheeks must hurt. "This is more than we could have ever dreamed of. I, I," Her breath catches as she tries not to cry. "I just can't wrap my head around how this is going to stay within the budget we had. I did my own research and prayed for maybe 1 or 2 programs a week but never imagined all of this. I noticed none of the slides discussed the financial pieces. So, while it sounds like a miracle, we really need to talk about price. We only have so much. While I would love to do all the things for all the kids, our center isn't exactly rolling in the dough." She trails off, her smile having dimmed slightly. Mine just grows wider.

"Well, Ms. Linda, I'm glad you brought that up." I take a moment to make eye contact with each person in attendance. Once I have reconfirmed their stance with beaming smiles and head nods, I turn back to her. "We believe in the next generation and what your center provides for them. We are grateful you have come to us for this chance to help the youth in the area do more than survive, but to thrive. Therefore, we are *all* offering our programs pro-bono. These kids already have a rough start and the last thing we want to do is potentially run out of funds and have to end it. They deserve stability and the opportunity to learn as much as they can from these programs as possible. We *do* ask that every 6 months we meet to decide which programs need to be expanded, and which ones are no longer creating interest. We can even discuss adding some things for summer to keep them active and busy while school's out. But, our priority is to ensure that we are always making the *kids* the focus."

By the time I have stopped speaking, tears are streaming down her face. Nick leans over and passes her a tissue box and she muffles out something between a laugh and a sob. The room is quiet as she gathers herself; all eyes on her. I take a quick glance around and see that she's not the only one overwhelmed with emotion. Bridgette steals a tissue and Gorge's chuckle is wet as he bats away a stray tear.

Linda finally gathers herself, mostly, before she begins laughing. She jumps up from her chair and makes her way around the room as asks each person for a hug. Nick asks for a handshake instead and she obliges without hesitation. But, Nick was all smiles through it. By the time she makes it to me, she wraps her arms around my neck. I lean down and wrap my arms around her and smile. "So, is that a green light?" She laughs out loud, pulls back, and says, "Yes, of course! Do you want to roll this out next year?" I look over her head meeting everyone's eyes before looking down at her. "Actually, we wanted to start November. It's a little over a month away but that way we can have some things started before Thanksgiving and Christmas break." Her ear-piercing scream echoes around the room and we all laugh as she jumps up and down, clapping her hands.

***

Twenty minutes later, the guys and I are cleaning the meeting room. Cory takes the trash to the dumpster outside and Nick closes down the computer and resets the screen. I wipe everything down and stack all of our contracts and paperwork together to be processed and filed. I sit down in one of the chairs and lean back, releasing an exhausted breath, and take a few minutes to just let it all sink in.

I don't even realize I'm smiling until Nick interrupts my thoughts, "That couldn't have been any better. Seeing everyone so excited, all of us with the same goal." He sighs and runs a hand down his face before revealing a huge smile. "It was fucking amazing."

He continues smiling at me and I nod, clapping his back, "Yup, we did it brother. Doesn't get much better than that."

We both sit in silence for a moment before Cory walks back in, collapsing into a chair near the door. He runs a hand down the back of his head a few times before facing us with a huge smile plastered on his face, his dimples on full display. "Well boys, we did it. Now what?" I look at him and grin while pulling out my phone. "*Now*, we call our girl."

I swipe open my phone, enter the passcode and find her name in Favorites. Clicking on the call icon, I quickly press the speakerphone icon so we can all tell her together. The phone doesn't even ring. A stab of disappointed pings in my chest before the voicemail beeps. I quickly gather myself enough to leave a message. "Hey Sweetness. Cory and Nick are here with me. We just wanted to let you know the deal is made and we owe it all to you."

Nick leans closer to the phone and adds, "We'd love to take you out to celebrate. Miss you."

Cory adds in "Have a great day, Pretty Girl. Miss you, more," grinning smugly at Nick who then flips him off.

"I miss you mostest, don't let them fool you." I say with a chuckle. "Have a good day. Call us when you can."

I end the call and look over at the guys, seeing that we're all grinnin' like fools. We take a beat, just basking in the overwhelming joy we have surrounding us. Between Annie and this youth program, things are feeling pretty amazing right now.

Five minutes later, my phone rings out and I see Vince's name before nodding and showing the guys the phone. I click the icon answer and then put it on speakerphone. "Hey, Everest. We just finished up our meeting with the youth center. You down to celebrate some time this week?"

The line is quiet. I don't hear anything at all. I glance down at the phone to make sure the call is connected. When I see that it is, I try again, "Hey, Vince, you there man?"

Nothing. Absolutely nothing. I glance at Cory who shakes his head and shrugs before looking at Nick. His brows are drawn down in a frown. He leans forward before saying, "Hey Vince. We're all here. Can you hear us? It's silent or muted or something."

Then we hear it; a deep stuttered inhale and a quick exhale. "Guys, I need you to come to the station. We need to talk." We all blanch in surprise at his tone. The pain in his voice mixed with the command of his words acts as a visceral shock to our systems.

"Vince, what happened? Are you ok?"

He ignores my question and gruffly responds, "Get here. Now. I'll tell you when you arrive." The phone hangs up with a click and we're all left speechless, glancing at each other in confusion. We know one thing for sure, whatever he's got to tell us, it's going to fucking suck.

5

Vince- One hour earlier

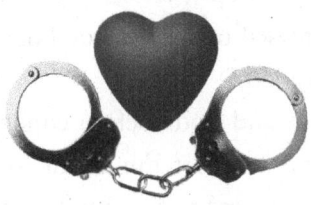

Walking into the interrogation room in front of Captain felt like I was being led to my death. *Why is he asking to speak to me here and why the hell does his face look somber?* My heart started racing and my palms were sweating. The hairs on the back of my neck and arms stand to attention, only serving to increase my anxiety.

I walk into the room, until I get to the center, and turn around. Captain slowly walks in and closes the door. I notice he has a file in his hand, his knuckles turning white as he inhales deeply. He makes eye contact and waves the hand with the file out towards the chair across the table. "Please, have a seat."

I respond immediately and without thought. "Tell me what's going on." I didn't mean to snap at him but this whole thing has alarm bells ringing in my head.

"Vincent. Sit. Down." He lashes out his command making sure there's no room for argument. I stare him down, flexing my jaw, before nodding my acceptance. I slide into the chair as controlled as possible, lean my arms on the table, and fold my hands together. My eyes focus on the chair in front of me for a beat before glaring over at my Captain; my boss. He raises an eyebrow and crosses his arm in challenge, the look on his face saying, "Really, Vince?"

That one look was exactly what I needed to remember that I trust this man. He wouldn't steer me wrong and whatever *this* is, protocol of some kind is probably the reason for the formalities. We've worked together for years and he's more like family to me than a boss. I close my eyes and breathe in deeply, releasing the tension and centering myself. When I have myself under control, I open my eyes and nod at him, "Sorry Cap. I'm good."

He eases his stance and nods before coming to sit in the chair across from me. "Vincent, what I'm about to tell you is *not* good. But, you need to keep your head or I will put you on forced leave indefinitely. Do I make myself clear?"

My eyes widen at the command. *Shit this is really bad. What the hell does he have in that folder?* I glance down at the folder as if it will suddenly become transparent.

After a tense moment, I steal another breath, squeeze my hands tighter, and force my gaze back to my Captain. "Yes, sir. I understand."

He eyes me for a minute before nodding. Sliding the folder open, he begins to unravel my world, one word at a time. "When you left my office that day, after showing me the information that connects Annie to someone in the Black Thorns, I've been cross-checking information. There were just so many possibilities. I agreed that it looked very promising but there wasn't anything concrete. So, I went with *your* gut, that this Lukas guy was the one harassing her."

He pauses and looks at me to signal that I'm following. I nod my confirmation and he continues. "I added her information to the Black Thorns files, to keep tabs on any new information that may come in. This morning, her name was flagged in our system."

My brows shoot to my head. "Okay," I say slowly. "So, is it something about what happened before or..." I trail off hoping he would hurry the hell up and fill in the blanks.

Instead, he opens the folder, and slides it to me. "No, Vince, *this* was called in last night. Annie's missing." He clears his throat and shifts uncomfortably in his chair before continuing. "Since I know there is a personal relationship there, I told them I would take care of the questioning."

It takes me a solid minute before I whip my head towards the back corner. Sure as shit, the red light is on. "Uh, you're interrogating me? What the fuck, Cap?" My voice booms through the room and I stand up so fast the chair flings into the wall behind me.

"Sit. Down. Now." His words are much harsher this time. "I'm not interrogating you. You should know better." His voice rings out with a mixture of disappointment and authority.

He stares me straight in the eye, and points to the chair before saying, "Now, sit down so we can get this part out of the way. I know you want to get out of here and find her but this has to happen first and you know it. So, sit down. Please." He looks furious but not necessarily at me. For me.

I breathe in as deep as I can, closing my eyes and holding for 5 seconds before releasing it. When I open my eyes, he still looks furious but I can also see everything else. Understanding, sympathy, and a determination to help.

I nod my head at him, bring my chair back to the table, and sit down so we can proceed. *Let's get this over with so I can find my girl.*

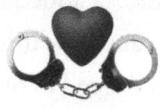

Three hours later, the guys and I are in the department waiting room, sitting in silence. Cap allowed us to break protocol and let me sit in the interrogation room with them and break the news. A kaleidoscope of emotions filled that tiny room today, suffocating each of us.

When it was time for Cap to question them, I had sit with the two who weren't being questioned in the waiting room. As Captain questioned each of them, the rest of us just sat, in ugly blue chairs, with the same cups of coffee we poured when they first arrived.

Nick is the last one questioned. When he's done, he walks in and plops down next to me with a heavy exhale.

After about five minutes, Captain pokes his head in the waiting room, "Vince, pack up and go home. I don't want you back until Wednesday." I absently nod then return to staring at the floor; arms resting on my legs, hands clutching my cup. I don't know how long we stay here; frozen in our minds, swirling between disbelief and anger. Sorrow and confusion.

"I gotta go. To work. I'm going to work." Cory's fragmented statement snaps us all out of our stupors just in time to see him rush out the door. Nick, Jenson, and I glance at each other before running after him. We catch up to him just as he steps into the elevator, and we all crowd in, bathing in silence once again. But, we can feel it. We can *all* feel it. The sickening stench of despair descends on us and we all start to unravel.

I suddenly find myself filled with the same sense of urgency Cory had. My clothes are too tight; everything is too tight. I start unbuttoning my uniform just as the elevators open. We all make our way through the station with a briskness one step below jogging. Once we hit the front door, I can hear the collective breaths we all take; like none of us were breathing right.

I head in the direction of my truck before turning around abruptly and shouting out, "Cory, don't you dare step foot in that gym. Family meeting, at home. I will call Frank and have him close for the day." I'm almost proud that I still managed to use my commanding voice when I feel like I am breaking apart. I turn back around, not even waiting for a response, knowing Nick and Jense can handle it.

The moment I reach my truck, I climb up into the cab, slam the door, and rip my uniform shirt off; leaving me in my white undershirt. I grab the steering wheel and begin to squeeze while rubbing my palms back and forth roughly. Closing my eyes, I take a deep breath, blow it out, and open my eyes again. *Get it together, Vince. Get home, get to your family. We figure this out together.*

Nodding to myself I stick my key in the ignition, snap my buckle in, and reverse out of my spot. Don't Give Up On Me by Andy Grammer plays from the radio and solidifies my resolve.

We will *find her. She* will *be ok. And I* will *put an end to Lukas Fucking O'Brian.*

6

Nick

The ride back to the house is stupidly silent. I feel like my skin is crawling. My stomach is sour, bile crawls up my throat, and I can't seem to get the buzzing in my ears to stop.

I don't remember getting home, or coming inside. As if on autopilot, I head straight for my playroom. Not my bedroom. The room where I can be free. Free of pain, free of judgment, free of shame and fear and the demons that plague me.

I heard what Vince said, and the questions his Captain asked, but it was like someone else was in my body. The whole thing was happening to someone else and I was just hovering above them, watching some poor bastard's heart break.

I blink and realize that I'm not only in my playroom, but I'm sitting on the bondage bench, feet resting on the shinpads. It doesn't surprise me, really. This is my favorite piece in the entire room. It calms me, centers me, makes me feel peaceful.

We commissioned it from a shop in the UK. The chest area contours in to allow for more comfortable arm positions. We can adjust the shin pads horizontally and vertically to suit the person, or the purpose, we use it for. Four different pairs of eyelets are positioned near the head, stomach, waist, and ankles. Additionally, there are belts that can wrap around the upper back, waist, both thighs, and both calves. The leather is a dreamy, creamy red. The reason why we bought it, though, is because the area where your hips go is specifically cut out for easy access from the other side. The leather coverings are 4 inches of comfortably thick padding, everywhere. Whether it's the head, chest, hips, or shins, the sub is well taken care of. Much better than that shitty wooden one we started with that barely had a scrap of cloth on the bench. The thicker padding allows the sub to accept longer punishments; and sweeter rewards. Edging is definitely the perfect line of pleasure and pain.

I've apparently turned on my hurting playlist as NF's Paralyzed permeates through the air. But, as I sit here, all I can think about is her. *Where is she? Did he take her? Why would he come back? What about her kids?* My mind rabbit holes, and I absently begin prepping the new hemp rope that came in.

I bought new rope last week because the other set was frayed and became dangerous. Safety is a big deal in BDSM and neither Vince nor I would want an accident to happen because we got lazy with checking that our materials could be used properly.

I've prepared our bondage ropes so many times, I could do it in my sleep. The act of breaking down the hemp strands allows it to become more flexible and softer. I start by threading the rope through one of the large eyelets hanging from the ceiling. I thread, twist, pull, untwist, repeat; until I get to the end.

Once the strands are perfectly frayed but not completely falling apart, I take the rope down and move toward the stainless steel counter on the long wall. The red lights littered around the room bounce off the counter and soothe my aching heart.

I lay out the rope, tying it to an eyelet on the right side and stretching it about a foot, while holding the remaining rope tight in my left hand. Grabbing my handheld butane torch, I flick it on and, when the flame turns blue, I slowly start to singe the frayed ends. I absentmindedly use repetitive, smooth motions, slowly uncoiling the remaining rope from my left hand as I go.

Eventually, I reached the end of the rope but, I just wasn't seeing it anymore. My mind was too lost in fear for Annie and what she may be going through. My brain processes the smell before the pain registers. I jerk my hand back and look at my thumb. It's red and angry and slightly bubbled up from where the flame touched it.

Tilting my head, I continue to examine my feelings. The pain, it feels good. It reminds me I'm still alive. *I've* lived through hell and Annie is *way* stronger than me. I know it. I have to believe that. I have to or I'll just fade again; letting my demons take me away.

The door to the playroom opens slowly and careful footsteps approach behind me. But, the burn, the marking on my thumb, is my only focus. I watch as the area blisters, feeling the pain spread. It's not until a hand slides down my right arm and squeezes my hand around the torch that I fully realize someone has entered.

I can feel him; feel the steady rhythm of his chest as he breathes in and out behind me. The calming presence that only Vince can bring surrounds me.

He brings his other hand down my left arm, gently applying pressure, until he reaches my hand. I watch in rapt attention as his hand moves to grip mine from under the side, making sure not to touch my newly acquired burn. We stay like that, suspended in this moment, until I finally begin to break.

My arms begin shaking, grip tightening on the rope and the torch.

I feel him lean his upper body against me, turning his head so he's buried in my neck and he inhales deeply. When he exhales, his breath skitters across my neck before he places a kiss at the base where my neck meets my shoulder. "I've got you, Pretty Boy. Let it go." He slowly moves his hand around mine and moves my thumb off the button, effectively turning off the torch. He wraps his hand around the torch, and gently pries it from my hand before tossing it on the counter with a thud. His hand comes right back, fingers weaving through mine as his hand rests on top, and squeezes.

He closes the tiny gap between us and presses himself closer as my whole body begins to tremble. "Good boy. Now, drop the rope and grab my hand." His voice is low but direct; calming. My body recognizes the command and I let the rope fall, moving my hand on top of his, before squeezing like it's the only thing keeping me together.

In a move that I don't fully process, he wraps his entire body around me from the back. His right arm banded tightly across my front and his left arm beneath it. The pressure behind me and in front of me, coming from the man who is my whole world, has me shattering.

My own demons from my past rise up to the surface. My fear for Annie, fear for myself, just fear; boils over until I can't breathe. My mind is lost, swirling with the worst possibilities and all the what ifs. I can feel my cheeks are wet, I can hear someone sobbing but I can't connect to them. Not now. Not yet. *I can't, I can't, I can't.*

I blink my eyes open slowly and take in my surroundings. My ass is numb and I feel like I have a hangover. Although, I know I didn't drink.

It takes me a minute before I realize I'm in my playroom. I vaguely remember coming down here and grabbing the hemp rope but the rest is lost. I look around, feeling confused and exhausted. I see the discarded rope, tied to the counter on one side and the rest hanging on the floor. *Why would I just leave it there?*

I begin looking over everything to give me some hint as to what happened. I'm suddenly hit with the realization that I am hot. So. Damn. Hot. And something heavy is wrapped around my chest. I look down and see two massive, bulging arms, tattoos skating up both. I grin, knowing exactly who is with me. My brain finally catches up as I feel the slow, measured, inhales and exhales telling me that he is asleep, propped up against the cabinet behind us.

I don't know how we ended up here but, as always, he knew I needed him. I take a deep breath and slowly start to unwrap him from around me. The movement causes me to hiss in pain, which wakes up Vince. I bring my hand up to inspect the area on and below my thumb. The red lights in the dark room make it difficult to really see it but *holy shit*, I can feel it.

Vince slowly unwraps himself from around me, grunting as he stretches. We both sit for a moment, embracing the silence. Finally, he looks deep into my eyes. His voice is filled with so much pain as he says, "I love you, Nick. I know I don't say it enough, but I do. You are my world. I can't lose you. So, I need you to talk to me. I need you not to shut me out. And I *need* you to not treat rope alone when your head isn't in it."

I grin, feeling equal parts embarrassed and cared for, and nod in agreement. He grunts and begins standing, stretching as he goes. Then, his hand appears next to my head and I look over my shoulder at him. His eyes are full of love, support, and understanding. I twist my body towards him, reaching my left hand out to place it in his. He slowly helps me to his feet and gently smiles down at me. "You good?"

I take a moment to take stock of my body and emotions before responding truthfully. "I'm tired, overwhelmed, scared, and my ass is now tingling since it fell asleep but, yeah, I'm good. Thank you, Love." I look into his whiskey brown eyes, raise my brow, and tilt my lips in a smile. His eyes light up as he smiles and leans in for a gentle kiss. When he retreats, he looks at me, kisses my nose, and steps back. "Come on, Pretty Boy. Let's go meet the others in the kitchen. We need to eat and then we need to talk."

Nodding quietly, I let him pull me back through the house, taking deep, controlled breaths on our way.

Reaching the kitchen, Cory is sitting at the table, head in his hands, and Jense is leaning against the island, staring down at the floor. They both look up as we enter and flick their eyes over my body checking for mutilation marks. I hold up my thumb and show it, knowing they will see it anyways, and quietly say, "It really was an accident. I zoned out when treating rope. Promise." I give a slight smile and they nod, seemingly convinced I didn't backslide into self-harm. But, I haven't done that in a long time. Not since the hospital stint after Amber. I've found other, more appropriate ways to relieve stress and the last thing any of us need is for them to worry about me.

I inhale deeply, straighten my shoulders and lift my chin. We need to focus on Annie and they won't do that if they are concerned about me. I walk over to the fridge, grab us all a bottle of water, and sit at the table across from Cory. "Alright Vince, what can we do?"

7

Jenson

Tension is so high in the room because we're still struggling to process. We just found Annie. She just opened herself up to us, allowing herself to take what she wants. *Where is she? How do we find her? Will she be ok?* "What can we do?" I voice my biggest question because it's all I want to focus on.

Vince clears his throat, takes a gulp of water and exhales roughly, "I don't know yet. Captain is allowing me to stay part of this investigation, for now. We have some ideas, if Lukas is the one that took her, that may help us find her."

He pauses for a moment, sighing before looking at each of us and saying, "But, you guys can't be involved. None of you are equipped for this." The kitchen echoes with sentiments ranging from "That's bullshit," and "Fuck off." We're all hell bent on finding her and we *will* be involved. Consequences be damned.

Nick looks Vince dead in the eye and calmly states, "You know the program I made for the gyms? The one that can pinpoint and track members coming and going?" Vince nods, remembering our little tech genius going above and beyond to make sure our facilities are safe. "Well, it might not be totally legal, but I can hack into street cams, doorbells, security systems, you name it. I would just pull her image from the gym and the program runs itself."

Vince quirks his brow in disapproval and Cory grins. "And how did you figure out you could do that?"

Nick blushes and drops his head, peeling the bottle label like he does when he's nervous. "Um, I accidentally did it a year ago." He clears his throat, shrugs his shoulders, and glances up at me through his lashes. "I was just messing around one day, not trying to do anything, specifically. Suddenly, all these various images were filling up the monitors and I realized some were from residential areas while others looked like security cameras around town." He shrugs again and lets out a self-deprecating chuckle. "I closed the program out once I realized what I did but, I know if I need to do it again, I can."

We all sit in silence looking at Nick; me smiling, Cory grinning, and Vince's face is contorted like he doesn't have a clue how someone just accidentally accesses hundreds of security cameras. I mean, I don't understand either but, if it helps us get Annie, I don't give a fuck.

Vince finally sighs before shaking his head, "Nick, you can't do that. That's federal prison time. No, there has to be another way." Nick quietly nods his head in acceptance before leaning back in his chair.

"Ok, so what do we do? Where do we start?"

For a moment, no one says anything. Then Vince slams his hand down, making us all jump "I got it!"

He runs from the room, leaving us all confused, and quickly

returns with his laptop in hand. He logs in and begins pulling up the server for his job. "Ok, if you guys want to help, we do it right. Cory, I need you to get the white board from the gym and bring it up here. Jense, we need a map of this area that reaches past Galveston. Nick, markers, magnets, and coffee. Lots of coffee." He says the last with a wink to Nick who grins back and gives him a salute before taking off.

"Wait. Galveston? Why Galveston?" I ask.

Vince doesn't miss a beat as he taps on the keys of his laptop. "Because this morning before I found out about Annie, we got a tip about a possible storage facility near Clear Lake. If that's where this bastard is holding his product, he may also have Annie there; or close by."

"Wait, you think he's going to sell Annie?!" Bile climbs up my throat and, judging by Cory and Nick's faces, they feel the same queasiness I do.

"No, I don't." He says matter of factly. "If he's been tracking her for years, he's not going to let her go. No; this is ownership, possession. Which means, he will keep her close to him. We find him; we find her." We all breathe a little easier, sort of, and jump into action.

In minutes we have everything set up. Vince is marking areas on the map where bodies have been dumped, the warehouses they know about, other places the Black Thorns have been associated with, and the newest possible location. He is definitely right. All the locations are curiously close to highways that lead to and from the Clear Lake area. Which, unfortunately, does dump into Galveston Bay and gives traffickers easy access to the gulf. *Fuckity, fuck, FUCK.*

"Ok, so let's back up and get our timeline. Annie left our place around 11pm." Vince makes a long line and begins to label as he talks out loud. "According to the intake, her mother called at 5:14pm when she went to drop off the kids. She hadn't heard from Annie all day. When she got to Annie's, her SUV was in the driveway, phone, keys, and purse were on the ground. So, it wasn't a robbery."

I can feel the anger zip through me, lighting my veins on fire. Fucking bastard jumped her. "Ok, so that means some time between, what, 11:20 pm and 5:14 pm, she was taken? That's an 18 hour window! How the hell does that help?" I don't mean to be snappy. I just need answers. We all do.

Vince quirks a brow at me before continuing, "Like I was saying, her phone, keys, purse were all there and her mother gave her phone over to the police to look through. It looks like the last call connected was with Lana."

"And Lana didn't say a fucking thing!" He cuts his eyes to me, silently demanding I shut up. I growl out my frustration, backing away, and running a hand through my hair, pulling hard. "Ok, ok, I'm sorry. Go on. Please."

Once he's satisfied I've composed myself, he continues. "So, I've put in a request for Lana's number. See what she remembers, if anything. We have no clue if the call was dropped or placed before. But, we won't know until I talk to her. Once I get her number, we'll go from there."

I nod my head, pacing around the living room before realization hits me. "Oh, God, the kids!" I choke on the sob that wants to rip free. The other three snap their eyes towards me.

Vince walks up, grabs me by both shoulders and leans his head down, forcing me to make eye contact. "Jense, listen to me." His command leaves no room for argument. "Her mother has the kids. They are safe. I promise. After I talk to Lana, I plan on calling Annie's mom. Just breathe for me brother; just breathe."

I close my eyes and take a deep inhale then push it out before doing it again. When I open my eyes, I can see we're both struggling. Heck, we all are. But he's right. I have to keep it together. The kids are safe, her mom is safe, and we will find Annie.

An hour later, Vince finally gets Lana's number. We have everything mapped out based on the information we currently have and are trying to fill-in the timeline. As we all crowd around Vince on the couch, he looks at each of us, silently communicating to not get involved and let him handle this part. We nod our agreements.

The call rings out on speakerphone, the phone sitting on the table in front of us. When it clicks to voicemail, we all slump. But, Vince doesn't let that stop him. He picks his phone up and sends her a text message explaining that he is a police officer and needs to speak with her urgently.

Not even two minutes later, the phone rings and he connects the call. "Hi, this is Lana. What's this about?" She sounds unsure and a little skeptical. *God, I hope she can help.*

Vince jumps right in, "Hey, Lana, this is Officer Daniels. Do you have a moment to talk?"

She's quiet for what must only be a few seconds but they drag on forever. Eventually, she cautiously responds, "O-kay. What's the reason for your call, Officer?"

Vince doesn't bother pussy-footin' around. He just jumps right in. "Look, in full transparency, my name is Vince. We have been hanging out with Annie a lot lately and we could use your help." Silence descends and I squirm in my seat, my heart-racing.

Suddenly, her voice perks up and she exclaims, "Oh! Vince. And Cory, Nick, and Jenson, right?" We all smile relieved that Annie has at least talked about us. "Yes, that's right. So, listen, we're all here, right now, but we need your help. It's about Annie."

Her voice takes on a flirty, teasing tone, obviously not reading the seriousness in Vince's tone. "Ooooo what can I help you with? I knew something good was happening between you all when I saw you with her at the club. But, I swear to everything unholy that if you hurt her, I will personally gut you, drive to Galveston, and dump you in the bay. You should consider yourself lucky she even agreed to date any of you. Let alone all of you. She *never* dates. She's very protective of herself and her kids. So please, *please* be good to her." She takes a breath after dumping it all out. Then, she sniffles a little before her voice turns back into happy and cheerful, "So, what can I help with?"

We all look at each other, now incredibly uncomfortable about what we have to tell her. Vince even looks like he's seconds away from ending the call. I clear my throat and jump in. "Hey Lana, this is Jenson. So, this call isn't a fun one. We really need your help. Have you heard from Annie lately?"

She takes a moment to consider before responding, "I spoke with her a little bit Saturday night. She was on her way home from being with you. And, she told me the good news. Why?"

We all look at each other before Vince nods for me to continue. "Lana, what time was that? Do you remember?" We can hear her moving the phone around. "I called her at 11:27. Why? What's going on?"

Vince finally switches into officer mode before answering. "Lana, Sunday evening, Annie's Mom reported her missing. No one has seen or heard from her since possibly you. Do you remember anything about that call that may be strange? Did she tell you about any of her plans for Sunday?"

We all wait with bated breath while Lana considers his question. Her voice breaks through the silence and we all lean toward the phone as she speaks in a calm, even tone; like she's walking us through her memory. "Saturday night, she told me you all made it official. She sounded happy, excited even. Then she told me to hold on because she had gotten home and the bluetooth messes up sometimes when she turns the car on or off. I remember I was doing my nails so I didn't really pay attention while I waited for her. But, I could hear her rummaging around like she was getting her things." She is quiet for a long time. My heart is beating so loudly I swear everyone must hear it.

"Holy fuck!" Her scream makes us flinch. Before any of us can question her, she proceeds. "I- I thought she just got disconnected. It sounded like she had tripped or something because I heard her say something like "Ow...fuck" but it was muffled. She can be a little clumsy especially when she has a few drinks. She doesn't drink much so, you know, it hits her hard so I just..." She's rambling now, not making any sense.

Cory cuts in to get her to refocus, "Lana. Stop! Take a breath."

She follows his command before trembling out a quiet, "Sorry".

"It's ok. Just focus. You said she may have said "ow" and "fuck" then what?"

She takes a steadying breath and continues, "Um, I figured she dropped her phone or something or maybe her phone died. I called out to her but she didn't respond. I waited another minute and heard some kind of grunt, like she was picking up something heavy. I heard a door slam. I figured it was her car door or something, and then it all went quiet. So, I- I hung up. Oh my God! I hung up!" Lana begins sobbing on the other end. "I ju-just figured she dropped her phone and got sidetracked. Sometimes she does that when she forgets her ADHD meds so, I just shrugged it off. I shrugged her off! I didn't know! I didn't know!"

Lana is completely melting down and while I know she must be crushed, she needs to know. "Lana, breathe. You are ok. You didn't know. But Lana, listen to me when I say this; are you listening?" I pause and wait for her to respond. Once she squeaks out a sobbed, "yes", I continue. "Lana you just helped more than you know. We have a timeline of when she went missing. Okay? So, you helped Lana."

She whines out a "thank you" and "ok, good" while starting to take deeper breaths. "Ok, I'm glad. You're right. What's next? What can I help with? Do you know who took her?"

Her rapid fire questioning mirrors those in my mind. Thankfully, Vince is on it. "Now, you save my phone number. If you hear or see anything, let me know immediately. Also, you may want to reach out to her mom and see how her and the kids are doing. I'm going to go over there later but I'm sure she would appreciate hearing from Annie's friends."

Lana takes in another shuddering breath before blowing it out and thanking us, promising she will call Annie's mom and get her other friends involved.

When Vince disconnects the call, we all sit there staring at each other, filtering through what we just learned. *She was taken. Standing right in her driveway, Annie was taken.*

Vince abruptly stands up and moves to the board, putting in the time of her disappearance before turning back to us. "Ok, I need to go see her Mom."

We all stand up to go but he stops us, holding his hands up. "Hold up. We can't all go there right now. We are so new in this relationship and have no idea what she has said to her mother; if anything. This woman is missing her daughter and watching her three grandkids. We don't need to overwhelm her with the knowledge that we're all dating her daughter. That isn't a conversation for *us* to have. Not right now. So, you all eat, get some rest if you can, and I will update you when I leave her house."

His words take a moment to process but Nick beats me to it, "Why are you going there? Instead of just calling?" I tip my chin towards Nick, agreeing with his question.

Vince sighs, rubs his hands down his face, and simply states, "Because this would be on official police business. I am still part of the case and it would help relax her to talk face-to-face, rather than over the phone."

He checks his phone and starts for the door. "I gotta go so I can try to get there before the kids get home from school. I definitely don't want to meet the kids without Annie's ok. But, I need to talk to her Mom. Let her know we're working on it and update her with what we've found out." He's mumbling the last bit to himself, nodding and walking out the front door without so much as a wave goodbye.

And, again, we are frozen, standing in the living room looking lost and broken with only one question filtering through our minds. *Now, what?*

8

Annie

My head is throbbing and I groan out. *Good Lord. I only had three glasses of wine over like 3 hours. Why do I feel like dog shit?* I didn't even feel remotely tipsy. I never would have driven otherwise. I've lost friends to drunk drivers so I'm very particular. That and I just don't like the feeling of not being in control. *Life, unfortunately, taught me that the hard way.*

I feel like my head is swimming. Scratch that. Not swimming; my head feels like an ocean crashing against jagged cliffs. *Fuck. Ok, Annie, you have things to do. Up, hydrate, Advil, clean. Let's go lazy bones.*

I make a move to roll over groaning as I go. Only, I'm stopped abruptly by something around my wrist. *What the hell?*

I begin fluttering my eyes open and immediately slam them closed. *Jesus. Why did it look like a spotlight was pointed right at me?* "Ok, An..." My voice is hoarse and raspy; my throat raw like I swallowed shards of glass. My tongue feels thick and foreign in my mouth and I work far longer than I should to try and swallow something, anything but, nope; dry as a desert.

I go to wiggle my arm again, trying to push through the grogginess and fog, and feel the familiar heaviness of metal clasped around my wrist. My eyes spring open as a deep gasp leaves my mouth. I'm immediately overwhelmed by the blinding light and it takes a minute before my eyes finally begin to adjust.

I glance around and find myself in a small, shallow bedroom. The bed, a queen judging from my position, takes up most of the space. My brain screams that I'm not safe and I start fighting against the cuffs, thrashing as my panic takes over. I wiggle and tug; the biting metal cutting into my skin. I can't figure out how I got here or why. *I can't do this. I can't be cuffed. I'm trapped. Oh shit! I'm trapped.*

My breaths come in faster and shallower. My head begins to feel fuzzy and my vision begins to tunnel.

Annie, breathe. You're ok. Nick's command in my head immediately has me stilling. I close my eyes and begin inhaling slowly and count to four, holding for four, exhaling for four. I do that three more times before my breathing returns to normal and I can think a little clearer. *Ok, first thing's first. Take in your surroundings, figure out as much as you can, then look for a way out.*

I begin by straining my head backwards to see what I'm connected to. Each hand is cuffed with a separate pair of cuffs. There appears to be circular hooks embedded in the headboard that attach to the other end of the cuffs. *What in the actual fuck?*

I look back down towards my feet to find cuffs around each ankle, leading down both sides of the bed. I lean over as far as I can but I'm unable to see where the cuffs are attached.

Blowing out an exasperated breath, I recenter myself on the bed. The Navy blue bedding gives nothing away. But, the interior...there's something so odd about it. The wood paneling around the room matches the door; and what might be a small closet. There also appears to be some cabinets in the same light oak stain. But, that's it. *That's it? That's fucking it? There's nothing here!*

I lie my head back down, exhaling raggedly. Tears prick my eyes but I fight them back as I try desperately to make the mess in my head make sense. Then, the hard reality comes crashing down. *I've been taken and I have no way out.*

That thought plays on repeat in my head like a scratched vinyl, quickly followed by a whirlwind of a dozen more. *Why is this happening? How long have I been gone? Are the kids ok? Oh my God! MY KIDS! Where are they? Are they here?*

This time, I can't calm my anxiety; can't fight the crushing weight of never seeing my kids again. *I can't stop. I can't breathe.* A distant part of my brain recognizes that my vision is tunneling, darkening around the edges but I can't get out. *I can't...*

I wake with a start, drenched in sweat. My eyes snap open and my head immediately starts pounding as I fight to keep the contents of my stomach firmly in place. A deep groan leaves my body as I reach up, trying to rub my face. But, I can't reach it. I'm stopped, again, by the metal cuffs.

The information I gathered during my last time awake smacks me in the face. And, I fall apart. This time, I welcome the tears, allowing them to tether me to the present. The pain in my heart reminds me I'm alive; for now.

What feels like hours, but is probably only minutes, I allow myself to just let it all out. To feel everything. I let myself think of everyone I left behind. My kids, my mom, Lana, the guys.

Shaking my head slowly, I focus on the guys; *my guys*. I finally opened myself up. And for what? I trusted them with my past. And now, I've disappeared and am drowning in more trauma. *Great, shortest relationship ever.*

I roll my eyes at my own ridiculousness. Then, I close them while taking deep, steadying breaths. The gentle sway of my body begins to relax my muscles and clear my mind. *Wait? Sway? What the hell is that? Why do I feel like I'm rocking?*

Now that I know something is definitely wrong, I *know* I wasn't drunk last night, I *know* someone took me, and I have a feeling, I know *who*.

Thoughts of Lukas plague my mind. *Why after all this time? Why did he really come after me? What did I do to him to deserve this?* Regardless of what he does with me, I hope Mom can get away; protect my littles. Their lives may have formed in the midst of my darkest moments but, I refused to let them see an ounce of it if I could help it. *If I* can *help it.*

And that's the thought I decide, right then and there, to hang on to. It completely changes my feelings of hopelessness to determination. I *can't* give up. I *can't* give in. *I'm* their Mom and, even though my mom would give them the world, it's not her job. It's mine, dammit. And I refuse to let this bastard take anything else from me.

Once my tears are dried and I have wrapped my entire being in determination, I feel confident that I can make it out of this. I let that confidence flow through me, steadying me. Now, I just need to figure out how long I have been here, and where the hell here is.

9

Vince

I'm on my way to meet Melissa. I just got off the phone with Cap, filling him in on what we learned from Lana and asking if he knew where Annie's mom was staying. I wasn't sure if she was staying at Annie's with the kids or picking them up from school and taking them back to her house across town. Captain confirmed she was staying at Annie's and also informed me that he has someone stationed outside the house at all times as a precaution. The latter made me breathe just a little easier so I could focus on the talk I'm about to have.

I pull into Annie's driveway and the memory of the last time I was here assaults me. Seeing her drop her walls, laughing and smiling like she didn't have a care in the world. She has clearly been through hell and back but, there she was, choosing happiness, choosing me, and eventually, choosing us. Damn, I miss her already. I need her back with me like I need my next breath.

I sit in the truck and take a moment to gather myself before putting my hat on and walking up to the door. The kids shouldn't be back from school for at least an hour so I hope I can be gone by then. I still don't want to give away our relationship without her here. Polyamory can be a lot for people to understand; many don't even bother trying to. And meeting her mom without her here already feels like it's wrong. They've been running for years and now her daughter has been kidnapped. She doesn't need anything added to her plate and I *definitely* don't want to meet the kids without Annie's approval.

I sigh heavily and knock on the door before I can start spiraling again. I stand there, desperately trying to hold on to my officer mask so my personal feelings don't bleed out. Not even 6 seconds later, a woman opens the door, just enough to poke her head through, and my breath stalls in my lungs. She is the older version of Annie. But, instead of platinum dyed, shoulder-length hair, she has a short brunette bob with caramel highlights. She has hazel eyes where Annie's are deep blue. But her smile, her nose, the way her eyes widen in surprise, the shape of her jaw and heart-shaped face; it's all Annie.

"Can I help you?" She asks cautiously. I quickly realize I've been staring at her like a dolt. I shake my head and chuckle before giving my best customer service smile. "Good afternoon, ma'am. I'm looking for Melissa Carson? I'm here about Annie." A lump clogs my throat as I say her name and I grimace at my inability to keep my feelings locked down.

Melissa's face drops then she opens the door wider, steps aside, and waves me in. I head into the kitchen and lean against the counter; the same one Annie leaned against when I heard her giggle for the first time.

"Do you have news on my Annie?" She asks hopefully. Her eyes are wide and pleading, and her hands tremble as she reaches into the refrigerator and grabs out two water bottles. She steps toward me and reaches out one of the bottles in offering. I thank her, twist off the cap, and take a long gulp before replacing the cap.

"Unfortunately, I don't have a lot more information to give you. We did confirm that she was taken Saturday night when she came back home. Her friend, Lana, had been on the phone with her but she thought Annie got distracted and just dropped her phone. And, since she's not one for late nights usually, Lana figured she'd call her later." I break eye contact as her eyes fill with tears. She angrily wipes them away before retreating to sit at the kitchen table.

"And do you know who? Or why? What do they want?" I clear my throat, knowing I will have to tell her about the messages Annie was getting. My chest tightens uncomfortably. *This is going to be a lot harder than I thought.*

I lift my hand out towards her and ask, "Do you mind if I sit?" She nods her head and waves me over. Once I sit, I take another gulp of water, inhale deeply, and exhale slowly. "Ma'am," she holds up her hand, cutting me off, "Please, call me Melissa." She smiles sweetly and I can't help but smile back. I nod my head in agreement before continuing, "Melissa, Annie and I have been working together for a little over a month. She had been receiving messages from an unknown number. Nothing too pointed but enough that it caused her to call in the department."

Her eyebrows furrow with worry, lips turning down in a frown. "Eventually, he called her a nickname that revealed his identity."

Melissa gasps, "Lukas!" Her eyes grow wide in terror, hands trembling as they move up to cover her mouth. I nod my head, confirming her fears.

After a moment, she gathers herself, breathing deeply, before placing her hands gently on the table in front of her. "Officer..."

"Daniels," I supply. "But, please call me Vince."

She smiles although it doesn't quite reach her eyes. "Vince...wait

Vince, Vince?" Her brows hit her hairline and her smile widens. "*The* Vince? As in the one my daughter has been hanging out with a lot during the day? The one who also has three friends that take over my daughter's lunch times, leaving her mother to fend for herself?" Her brow quirks, waiting for a response.

I clear my throat, take another swing of water and fumble with something, anything to say.

Suddenly, she bursts out laughing. "I'm just messin'. But, *are* you that Vince?" Her eyes twinkle with mischief and her smile makes me feel like she isn't mad, or judgmental. Just curious.

I clear my throat, "Yes, ma'am. I was working on her case and then we, uh, met out, in public, with my friends. Well, family. We've been together since high school. Anyway, we all started talking and hanging out and we just kind of, kept doing it."

My eyes widen with how that sounded and I start shaking my head before my brain supplies me with a way to correct myself. "I mean, kept hanging out, that is. She, uh, goes to the gym we own and I guess Nick and Jense ran into her there and sweet talked her into lunch."

She whistles with a grin and I can't help but smile. "Well they must be real smooth to talk her into anything that doesn't have to do with her kids, or me, or Lana." She chuckles and shakes her head with a smile. Then, those knowing eyes turn towards me and I suddenly feel like I'm in high school again, sitting in my dad's office after we got caught egging a house.

Her face relaxes and her smile settles into a slight grin as she searches my face; for what, I don't know. Thankfully, she breaks the tension before I start to really sweat. "Well, Vince, I'm glad she found you boys. I know she's had a lot of things happen to her; good, bad, terrible. But, I'm glad she's letting herself open up again." She reaches her hand across the table and lays her hand on mine before continuing, "Please find my baby. Bring her home to us, and then treat her like deserves."

She pauses for a beat, searching my eyes, before raising her brow, grinning, and adding, "All of you." With that she squeezes my hand, jumps up and asks if I want anything to eat. I'm so stunned by her not-so-subtle admission that she knows *exactly* what the guys and I are to her daughter, that I fumble for a response.

I see the time display on the stove and realize I'm cutting it close. I decline her offer for food and ask her to keep me updated if she hears anything. She adamantly agrees and walks me to the front door and opens it for me to walk out. I step out on the porch before turning around to face her. "Ma'am, Melissa, it was a pleasure to meet you. I absolutely loathe the conditions, and I'm sure Annie will have her own thoughts about this but, I want you to know, I am doing *everything* in my power to find her. We all are; not just the PD but the guys, too."

She smiles so wide and leans up to pat my chest. "I know you are. I appreciate you. Whatever you need, you let me know. I want my daughter home and the kids need their mom."

With that, I remember, "If you don't mind me asking, I haven't met the kids, and I don't want to take that choice from Annie so I know I have to scoot but, what have you told the kids?"

Melissa folds her arms over her chest, tears filling her eyes, as she shakes her head. "I didn't know what to say. So, I told them their Mommy had to go out of town for work. She has to travel occasionally, definitely with way more notice, but it's at least something they're familiar with. Josh and Cheyenne cried wondering why she left without saying goodbye. They want to FaceTime her but I keep making excuses. We've just," She sighs heavily, wiping away the steady stream of tears that have started trailing down her cheeks. "She worked so hard to protect them as much as possible. She's lost so much, been through so much, but she wants to shield them from it all so badly. I-I have a feeling she was even lying about the kids' conceptions but, I know enough. She's a strong woman, Vince. I know she is. But she's been through too much already."

Her wide eyes, shimmering with tears, bore into mine as she says, "I know God can heal, but sometimes he sends people to help us with it. Maybe He knew she'd need more backup than just her own mom this time." She releases a self-deprecating chuckle under her breath and I can't help but smile.

"Melissa, Annie is the strongest, sweetest, most amazing woman I have ever met. I don't want to think the worst of where she is, but I know for a fact that she will not have to be alone when we find her. And we *will* find her. We *will* get her back. And we *will* help you put the pieces back together; if she wants us to."

She smiles through her tears and nods. "Thank you, Vince. For everything. Keep me updated, please." I tip my hat and smile wide as I say, "Will do. Take care and don't let the kids run you over." She laughs and shakes her head before waving goodbye.

I head back to my truck, feeling more determined than ever. Melissa is getting her daughter back, the kids are getting their mother back, and we are getting our girl back. Now to head back and figure out our next move.

10

Annie

As a kid, my friends and I would talk about which super power we would want. At the time, I chose invisibility. It's better to not be seen. No one can judge you, hurt you, break you. But, as I got older, I realized that dissociation was really the best super power.

I started realizing my power when Lukas' temper started to scare me; around three months after we started dating. I slipped and dropped a plate of food. He went from zero to sixty before I could even start to clean it up. He yanked me around by my arm to face him, nose to nose, and started screaming at me. He yelled at me for being so clumsy and a complete screw up, then let me go with a slight shove, sending me to the floor. It was the first time I ever felt fear in his presence.

Not liking confrontation, I just sat there cleaning the mess, quietly sobbing.

At some point, I came back to my body and realized I had scrubbed the entire kitchen clean, but didn't remember any of it. I thought it was weird but didn't think too hard about it.

I remember going to the living room and finding him on the couch watching tv. I stood there for a moment and just watched him; beer in his hand, and looking relaxed as ever.

Deciding to not rock the boat, I quietly told him I was going to bed. He looked over at me, confusion contorting his stupid face, and reached his hand out to me. I stared at it for a second before hesitantly putting my hand in his. The moment we touched, he whipped me into his lap, and began nuzzling my neck. "I'm sorry, kitten. I didn't mean to yell." His hand was rubbing up and down my thigh and I couldn't help the shiver of uncertainty that ran through me. "I had a rough day but I shouldn't have yelled. You just need to be more careful." I gave him a fake smile while nodding at him; telling myself it would be fine. I mean, we all have bad days so, no harm done. Little did I know, our days would be filled with more bad than good.

His temper grew, week by week, and I let him down more and more. I found myself 'coming back into my body' frequently before I even realized I was dissociating.

Eventually, I began dissociating during other times; not just when his temper was high. It started happening when we had sex while he was angry, or drunk. Then, it occurred every time we were intimate. It's like he went from trying to at least make it feel decent for me, to just doing it to get off.

Ice cold water unexpectedly snaps me out of my memories. I gasp and sputter, trying to breathe through the mixture of water in my mouth, and the cold seeping into my bones. "Get up, Princess. Time to go."

A man I have never seen before stands at the foot of the bed, scowling down at me. He has a scar on the left side of his face running from his hairline, through the end of his brow and down to his lip. And not like a little scar. A big, thick, scar that is pink and angry looking.

The man isn't as tall as Vince but his muscles bulge like he lifts weights for a living. He is the epitome of terrifying. He sneers at me before snapping, "I said get up, Bitch!"

I jump and realize that I didn't process what he was saying. "I, um, I'm sorry, what?"

He sighs impatiently before reaching down and grabbing my ankle, ripping me off the bed. I land on the floor with a thud and groan as the air is knocked out of my lungs. *Dammit. I didn't even know he had uncuffed me. When the hell did that happen?*

My body finally catches up with my mind and I scramble upwards, using the bed to help me stand. I have no idea how long I've been here. Long enough that my stomach is actively screaming and my legs tremble underneath my weight.

I rise to a stand in front of Mr. Angry Face and stare up at him. "Where are we going?" My voice is hoarse and scratchy from lack of use, and probably from whatever they had given me before.

Mr. Angry Face just raises a brow before wrapping his arm around my bicep; squeezing hard. I yelp in pain, knowing for a fact there will be bruises there tomorrow. He twists us around quickly and shoves me up the stairs, causing me to stumble. I recover as quickly as possible and make my way up the stairs.

As soon as I hit the top of the stairs, I see the back of what must be a kitchen that opens up to a decent sized living room, dimly lit by the ten or twelve recessed lights running parallel across the entire space. But, it's not the kitchen and living room, decked out in white cushioned furniture and polished oak cabinets that steals my breath.

Oh, no. What causes me to freeze are the windows around the entire room. Or should I say, the fucking dark abyss *outside* of the windows around the entire room.

"What the hell? Where are we? Why am I here? What do you want?" My voice has definitely become frantic and I couldn't keep the tremble out of my voice. I try turning back to face him but the feel of something hard and small hits my back hard enough that I wince and freeze in my tracks. "Shut. Up." He growls out. The unmistakable click of a safety echoes around the space and I realize just how much shit I am truly in.

I slowly raise my hands in a peaceful gesture and nod my head once. He nudges the gun in my back a little more to push me forward. I slowly shuffle my feet through the kitchen and living room. The large windows surrounding us show that we were definitely on the water.

Just as I reach the door, the guy's radio or something crackles. "Pulling up in 2 minutes. Get the merch ready to move."

A moving light beam appears in my periphery along the left side of what I'm assuming is a boat. Then another, and another.

Suddenly the door is opening in front of me. I stagger backwards with a startled shriek, digging the gun deeper into my back. I hadn't even noticed lights coming from the other side; or, hell, from thin air.

"Move!" Mr. Angry Face barks out, making me jump. The guys in front of me step back through the door and to the side, waving for us to pass. I walk forward, stepping out onto the main deck on the back of a huge boat. I mean, I walked through it, I knew it was big. But, looking around me now, I can see exactly how huge this thing really is thanks to the bright ass light shining down on it from above us.

He shoves me to this side of the deck and grunts, "Hands behind your back." I silently obey and feel rough plastic slide around my wrists before tightening; holding them together. *Ah, zip ties. Awesome.*

He steps back, putting the gun back in my spine before saying, "Stay put. Head down. Don't move. Don't talk." My eyes widen with fear and tears begin to spill over. *Holy shit. Are they going to dump me out here? In the middle of the water?* I hang my head and sob silently.

Suddenly, there are sounds of footsteps, grunting, and water moving loudly. I chance a peek through my lashes to see a giant spotlight shining on a black cargo ship. The ship appears to be coming up on the back of the boat; but perpendicular to it.

I try controlling my breathing as my overactive imagination takes the stage. Images play through my mind like a horror film: the bigger ship colliding with ours, me falling in the water, hands zip-tied behind me, no way to ever see my kids.

The possibility of never seeing them again rips a sob from my throat. Tears are flooding my face; the pain in my heart becoming so unbearable that I can't breathe.

A man to my left suddenly shouts orders, bringing me out of my anxious thoughts. I can hear at least ten people walking around, grunting, and someone calling out numbers. I blink my eyes a few times to clear out the tears and peer over to my left side. I see the ginormous black ship is now sitting right behind the deck, with a large door opened inwards. Men are passing huge wooden crates from our boat to the other. But then, the boxes stop, and in their place is something much worse.

"What the hell is this? Why do they have leashes and why are they barely keeping their eyes open? What's wrong with them? Where are they going?" My words carry over the rocking of the boats and the wind whipping across the water.

I begin to turn towards Mr. Angry Face but, before I can even make it half way, I'm struck in the head by something hard; and my world fades to black.

11

Vince

It's been four days. Four days since we saw Annie; since we made her ours. Four days since she was taken.

On Wednesday, the guys talked me into letting Nick run his program to search for Annie. After a day of nothing. I let him use Joey and Lukas' pictures, from various sites, to track them down and the Clear Lake area lit up like a damn Christmas tree. *Not that I would tell the PD that.* There are a handful of places that they both visit frequently, so those are our first targets. Nick is still running the trackers and will update me if he gets any more hits.

Today, we're meeting with the Clear Lake PD and splitting into teams to cover the areas we have had hits on; using both legal and illegal methods. In the last 36 hours, we have connected a lot of possible locations based on tips and informant information.

After an hour in traffic, thanks to the never-ending construction in this city, I step out of my truck and into the disgusting parking lot. Between high humidity, temps in the 90s, and the rain pouring down, it appears the weather decided to literally dampen my already shitty mood.

Three other trucks and a small SUV pull in next to where my partner, Nate, and I parked. Eight of us are on this little excursion. We paired up and decided on taking our regular vehicles to keep our activities discrete.

Once out of the vehicles, we glance at the light blue building standing tall on stilts with cars parked underneath. While it's not seen too frequently inland, where we are, stilts are common. Being right on the water means flooding is probable so most homes and offices are lifted using thick beams. The fading paint around the building is also typical for this area given the breeze whipping salt water through the air.

I look at each of the officer to make sure we're ready and nod towards the building, silently commanding them to follow. We make our way to the right side of the building, where a staircase leads to the PD door. The stairs creak under our weight but we continue stomping upwards. At the top of the stairs is a small wooden deck that wraps around the front as a balcony.

The door in front of the stairs opens up as I reach out my hand, revealing a tall, lean man. He's about my height, maybe mid-twenties, and definitely spends more time outside than I do; given his tanned skin.

His smile widens as he moves aside and waves us in. "Welcome to Clear Lake Shores, we have everything set up in the conference room. Just straight through to the back." He points across the long building area to a room. Through the large windows lining the wall, we can see a huge conference table with multiple evidence boxes stacked on it.

I gave him a polite smile and a nod of my head before leading the guys through the room; weaving between tables and desks. As we approach the windowed room, a door to the left opens and an older gentleman steps in. The scent of stale tobacco wafts off of him as he stomps his black boots on the mat, shaking the water off of his bright orange poncho.

Once the large door slams shut behind him, he looks up, and grins as he takes my hand with a firm shake. "Officer Daniels. We've been expecting you. I'm Chief Donnelly."

After he shakes everyone's hand, and I make introductions, he steps into the conference room and waves us in. "So, we have all of the information we have acquired plus the files you sent over." I nod before replying, "Thank you. I sent over everything we got from West Texas, too."

With just those spoken words, we started combining our timelines and information. We spend hours pouring over all the information, and lining it out in a way that makes sense; like outlining the border of a jigsaw puzzle.

It was tedious but I can feel how much closer we are to taking these assholes down. At times I can't even remember, lunch, then dinner, were dropped off. After dinner, we were finally ready to plan.

Chief agreed on us splitting into groups. We would have three or four in a group and check out each area on the map marked with a yellow dot. All of us from HPD would go in civilian clothes to scope out the area and ask questions, posing as if we're interested in whatever service they provide; marina boat slip, two storage businesses, and a bait and tackle shop. CLSPD is pretty small and would need a few people to stay around the office in case of other emergencies. The rest will double check on Joey sightings. This area is huge for tourism so the officers in this PD would stick out to the locals who live here.

Once the plan is in place, we decide to start early in the morning and agree to leave for the night. Leaving the station at 9:00pm. we quickly make our way to the hotel down the block to get some sleep.

It's nice, as far as this area goes. It's also close to the Kemah Boardwalk so we blend in like every other tourist; but we stagger our check-in to ensure we don't attract too much attention.

Once in my room, I throw my bag down and walk into the small bathroom. I don't need much but I am kind of a big man so I'm thankful that the bathroom is not only large enough for me to walk into, but has enough room to move around a little. The worst bathrooms for guys like me are the ones where you open the door and immediately fall into the toilet. Having to do acrobatics across the sink just to close the damn door all the way is not my idea of fun.

I open the curtain and turn the shower on, just above scalding, and begin to strip down. I don't need to see the mirror to know what I look like. Even with the copious amounts of coffee I've consumed, black bags line my eyes and I have been basically walking around with a resting asshole face.

Thoughts of Annie and what she has already been through, mixed with worst case scenarios of what she is currently going through, play through my mind. It makes my stomach swirl like a giant whirlpool. I am in a consistent state of fear, exhaustion, and rage.

I step into the shower and face the spray. Leaning my hands on the wall, I drop my head forward and allow the burn from the water to take over my body. Rivulets of water cascade down my face, swirling with tears I didn't know I released. The emotions pour out of me; and I let them. I need to be clear and open for tomorrow to work, for us to get what we need to find Annie. So, I let it all out. I sob, I pull at my hair, I growl in frustration; I release it all in hopes that it helps to refocus me.

Eventually, my fingers prune and I have emptied myself of all my big emotions. Taking a deep breath, I turn off the water and snatch a towel off of the bar before stepping out and drying off.

Walking out into the bedroom, I open my bag, grabbing some fresh briefs and my toothbrush and toothpaste. After pulling up my briefs, I grab my phone and sit down on the bed. I call Nick and am immediately relieved when he answers before the second ring finishes. "Hey! How's it going? I knew you would be busy but I've been on edge all day. Are you ok? Any news?" I find myself grinning at his rambling.

For a moment, I couldn't figure out how to respond. All of a sudden, I just blurt out, "I love you, Pretty Boy." My voice cracks at his pet name.

There's a long pause before he responds, almost too quietly to hear, "I love you too, Vince. Wh-what's going on?"

I shake my head before remembering he can't see me. "Nothing new to report. I just," I sigh and rub at the top of my head, still wet from my shower. "I miss you. I know we're all hurting and we've all been reeling about losing Annie but," I trail off, squeezing my eyes shut and absently rubbing my chest.

"But what?" He pushes.

"This is going to sound stupid but I *feel* her Nick. I swear I feel her, here, somewhere close. I don't know if it's my own expectations and hopes or what but it has been physically difficult to breathe since we got here." I usually don't act this, *feely*, but it's all I can do to stay here and not go out and start tearing through the city in search of her.

Nick takes a moment before responding, "I get it, Love. I felt it the moment we narrowed down the search to the Clear Lake area. It *feels* right; feels good. Fuck, it feels terrifying, too. But don't let it cloud you, Vince. You can do this. I know you always carry the burdens for us and all of your cases, and now Annie but, Vince, we need you to concentrate just on Annie. Okay? You go out there tomorrow and do what you do best; find the bastards and make 'em pay. Then bring home our girl."

I could hear how hard Nick was trying to convince us both and I had to smile. "Thank you, Nick. You're right. Listen, I gotta get some sleep but, I'll message you in the morning before we get started."

We say our goodbyes before hanging up, then I connect my phone to the charger. I quickly head to the bathroom to brush my teeth before flipping off all of the lights. As I settle into the flat pillows and scratchy sheets, I go over tomorrow's plan again. Then, my mind fills with thoughts about Annie, Nick, Annie's kids, and Melissa.

It takes me a couple of hours before I finally fall asleep, and thankfully I dream of our future. One *with* Annie and her kids.

12

Annie

During the last thirteen months with Lukas, we only had sex when he was apologizing for an outburst or when he was drunk. Sex has always been something I just did as my duty as his girlfriend. I used to only sort of dread it. Now, I hate it more than I hate writing essays for my college classes.

Although my medical conditions don't seem to upset him anymore, he's stopped trying to make it feel good for me and he damn sure has stopped trying to get me wet before starting. Unfortunately, that means it's way more painful than it used to be. Like, sitting on ice packs afterwards due to friction, type of painful. Usually, I end up wiping away blood but, I'm sure it's normal for women to tear.

I've always been worried about making up for my short-comings, so I never complained, and definitely never told him how awful it was for me. It was my fault I was broken so there was no reason to make him upset about it. Thankfully, he never noticed me dissociating, either. He would just fuck me, grunt "love you," and fall asleep shortly after. Then I would sneak off to the bathroom and clean up, feeling gross but relieved I could make him happy; that he still loved me.

On our one year anniversary, I went from involuntarily dissociating to honing it; using it to actually help me. I'll never forget looking up at his ice-blue eyes, begging me to try something new.

> I walked in on him watching porn on his laptop and he's decided he wants me to watch, too. I don't mind. Porn hasn't really been my thing but, whatever. I know guys tend to have higher sex drives so if that's what he wants, I'm fine with it. What I was not prepared for was a woman getting railed in the ass. Watching her body open for them was interesting, to say the least, but I couldn't shake the uncomfortable feeling weighing down on me.
>
> "You want to make me happy, right Kitten? I mean, we're happy together so that means we do everything for each other. Even if it takes some getting used to." Lukas has his hands on my cheeks, rubbing his thumb across my lips.
>
> "Of course I want you to be happy, Lukas. I'm just, I don't really have a lot of experience outside of you when it comes to stuff like that. I know it will hurt and I'm scared." I whimper out, sitting on the edge of his unmade bed.
>
> Lukas' brows pinch as his scowl begins replacing his gentle smile. "Dammit, Annie. It's fine. Why is everything always about you? Why can't you do this one thing for me? It's not that bad. People do it all the time. And, you take it in the puss well enough when I

spit so what's the difference?" His voice steadily raises with each word spoken and I can feel my heart breaking; pieces of my soul flying away. I don't want to be selfish. I want him to want me. And, he's right, a lot of other people do it. Maybe it will be fine.

I plaster on a big, fake smile and nod, "You're right, Baby. I trust you." The moment the words leave my mouth, fear tingles down my spine.

Little did I know, today would be the day that I officially learned how to control my dissociation; making it my ultimate super power and allowing me to escape the shame and the pain that would follow.

Intense pain radiates across my right cheek and I scream out as I'm wrenched out of my nightmare. Sadly, it appears I'm still living in one.

I blink my eyes a few times, clearing the tears so I can take in my surroundings. It takes me a moment to realize that I'm staring out at steel bars. Like actual fucking bars. The pounding in my head isn't making my perusal any easier but I'm certain that's what they are.

I close my eyes and go to press my hand against my temple but am stopped by the familiar feel of metal cuffs; again.

I may not have ever been to jail but I'm pretty sure it would be brighter than this place. There seems to be a dim light emanating from somewhere to the right of the...*cell*. Across from this space, there is nothing but a dirty, red bricked wall. "Fuckity, fuck," I curse loudly in the space.

"Oh, kitten, hearing those words from your mouth is *so* sexy." I jump at the hauntingly familiar voice of the man I once loved, coming from behind me. I try turning my head around but can only see just over my shoulder. I realize the cuffs are not only on my wrists behind my back, but also around my ankles, securing me to what looks like a wooden chair.

"L-Lukas? Is that you?" I tried to keep the fear out of my voice but I know I failed miserably.

Heavy footsteps start from somewhere behind me. Not too far, maybe 6 feet-ish, but too close for comfort. Lukas makes his way, painfully slowly, around my left side. When he stops, diagonally from me on my left side, the lights from the hall light up his face and make him look almost sinister.

The man I'm looking at is so damn similar to the man I once knew; but he's harder, darker, scarier now. His ice-blue eyes are the same but they look void of any emotion other than pure hatred. His sandy brown hair is longer now, sitting just below his ears and it looks like he's been running his fingers through it for the last two weeks. He's grown a full beard instead of a goatee; letting it grow around his top lip and falling just below his chin.

He's totally shirtless, something red splattering his torso and chest. The red brings out the dark ink swirled on his chest, neck, and hands. He has big, black, entwined vines lined with thorns starting at his collarbone and wrapping around his back, ending at the opposite end of his other collarbone. The thorny vines are about 2-3 inches thick. His lower abdomen has big, chunky numbers 666 spanning from one side of his hip to the other. It's like, once he decided to ink, he covered the whole damn area in that design; even if it looked stupid.

His chest and stomach are about the same they were before. Not necessarily a 6 pack but not pudgy either. His arms must be where he spends his time because those are defined, firm, and I can see every little twitch as he takes me in. He's wearing black suit pants and shiny ass shoes. I know my facial expression shows every bit of confusion I feel as I compare the man I knew to the one standing before me.

We stare at each other, for God knows how long. I can already feel the disappointment and shame growing in me as his mouth and nose curl in disgust.

When the silence gets to be too much, I take a deep breath in, and prepare to face my greatest demon. "Lukas. Why am I here? Why did you come for me after all this time?" I can't fully wrap my head around it. I am no one. And, looking back now, I can absolutely tell how stupid I was, how ridiculous our relationship was, and that there was no love there. *So, why come for me? Why not just move on?*

The questions are whirling in my head as I search his eyes for something, anything to help me. But, his eyes are cold, cruel, and black with disdain. "Why?" He repeats, "Why?!" His voice booms through the small cell and I flinch, reminding me of the pain in my temple and across my cheek.

My lip starts to tremble as fear courses through me. His dark chuckle echoes around me and he begins moving closer. He bends down so his face is right in front of mine, our noses almost touching, before whispering, "Why would I waste my time with you? Why would I possibly give a shit about the woman who put me behind bars?"

As he says the last word, a searing pain rips through me, causing me to scream out in agony. When the first tears fall, I move my head down to see the source of my pain. A knife handle is sticking out of the top of my left thigh, just to the left of the middle. It takes me a moment to breathe through the pain and nausea as my brain kicks into overdrive.

"Look at *me*, bitch." Lukas roughly grabs me by my jaw and lifts my eyes to meet his. While blurry from tears and dizziness, I can see the delight in his eyes at the pain he has caused.

My voice shakes uncontrollably as the only words that I could think to say tumble out, "I- I'm sorry." Did I know what I was saying sorry for? *No.* Did I actually think I had anything to be sorry for? *Nope.* Was I going to say anything he wants to hear to get me out of here? *You bet.*

His laughter is dark and sinister, reminding me of what The Candyman sounded like when he laughed. I blink back the tears and focus on pushing out the pain. Taking a deep breath, I re-open my eyes to find his glare settled on me. With all the strength and false bravado I could muster, I ask, "What do you want from me?"

He lets the question hang in the air long enough that I begin to worry I didn't actually say anything.

Finally, he smirks, a devilish gleam in his eyes, and moves back into standing position, making him literally tower over me. When he speaks again, his tone is steady, controlled, and he enunciates every single word. "I want you to feel how I have felt every day for the last ten years. You will pay, through blood, sweat, and tears, and then, when I think you have some kind of understanding of what you did to me, I will kill you before taking your brats and raising them to be my good little soldiers."

He pauses for a moment before his smile widens and he reaches his arms out wide, "After all, kids need a daddy."

My eyes are as wide as saucers. Not from punishing *me*. No, he can do whatever he wants with me; but not my kids. "No, please no! Leave them alone. Let Mom care for them. They need her and she needs them. Please, I'll do anything. Just leave them alone." I feel like I'd beg on my hands and knees if I wasn't strapped to this damn chair.

His entire aura darkens as his grin grows and he levels me with a hard glare. Then, he steps back. "Brute!" he yells out towards the hall outside the cell. "Give Annie our VIP treatment." As he ends the command, leaving no room for argument, a huge bruiser comes walking in.

If bulldogs were humans, this guy would be one. His right eye is scarred over, like a skin flap was placed there so no one has to look in his eye socket. Unlike Lukas, Brute is wearing dark jeans and a blue t-shirt under a huge leather jacket. His hair is a military style buzz cut and there looks to be a jagged scar, splitting his bottom lip; like it wasn't stitched properly. His biceps are as big as bowling balls and

I'm pretty sure his thighs could squeeze a watermelon to the point of exploding.

This must be Lukas' enforcer and, I have to say, I can see why. Just looking like that must have people running in the opposite direction. If his 'treatments' are half as scary as he looks, I get it. I totally see why he was chosen.

I can feel my body tightening with fear. I look back at Lukas as he casually walks back through the opening of my cell. The door slams shut; the sounds of the metal shaking reverberates through the space.

Lukas takes another step away, before stopping and turning back towards me. A devilish smirk crawls up his face as his eyes bore into mine. "Welcome home, kitten. I'll come back in a couple of days to introduce you to your new family. Then you'll learn how to earn your keep. *Everyone* has a part to play." With that, he winks and saunters off.

I follow the sounds of his footsteps until a large, irritating squeak sounds out, then slams closed. *Must be another door.* I take a deep breath, closing my eyes and trying to control the emotions warring inside of me.

Suddenly, the cuffs around my wrists are being released. *Holy crap. How did that big bastard walk around without me noticing?* My arms immediately collapse at my side from lack of use. The tingles racing through my arms are annoyingly painful. Brute bends down, close to my ear and roughly says, "Don't try anything." Before I can respond, he's unlocking the cuffs from my ankles, and dumping me out of the chair. My knees smack the unforgiving concrete floor and I realize I'm looking down at a drain hole. *Oh dear God.*

Before anything else could work its way through my mind, I'm yanked up by my hair. I scream out in pain as he hoists me up to stand. Brute quickly makes work of tying a rope of some kind around my right wrist; tightly. My mind finally catches up and I decide to try something; anything.

I lash out at Brute with my left hand, clawing him across the face. My body is still so sluggish from whatever they dosed me with before; then knocking me out again. He drops my other hand, rope already tied to it, and backhands me with a snarl. Sparks fly across my vision as the sting blooms across my face. I'm sure I now have matching prints on my cheeks. I don't even stop to care.

I continue with a punch to his gut, briefly excited for the grunt it earns me, before stepping back to kick him in his face while he's bent over. Just as I'm about to connect, his big, burly hands wrap around my ankle, stopping me mid-air, before roughly shoving me back. My left leg buckles under the pressure and I land on my back with a whoosh of air leaving my lungs; just as my head smacks the floor.

My ears are ringing and my vision is blurry. I can't focus on anything until Dickhead appears above me, wrapping a meaty hand around my throat and yelling something at me. The ringing is too loud for me to understand his words but, based on his facial expression, it's safe to say I pissed him off.

He quickly flips me on my stomach, pinning my left arm underneath me and pressing my head to the floor. The scent of mildew and sweat fills my nostrils as he climbs on my ass. Then he wraps his legs around mine, ensuring I can't get up no matter how hard I try. He yanks the rope tied to my right wrist and bends my arm behind my back before yanking out my left arm from under my body. I can feel his body vibrating with rage as he wraps my other wrist; just as tightly as the first. I try tugging and, although it appears my wrists aren't tied together, I still can't wiggle my hands free. Like, maybe they were tied with two separate ropes.

Suddenly, he yanks both ropes, causing my arms to jut out behind me. Then, in a move I'm not sure makes sense in my head given his size, he whips his body around, planting himself back on my ass, but facing the opposite way. I feel the tug on my wrists telling me he still has control of them. I try to see what he's doing but all I can tell from my position is that he is, in fact, facing the other way, and bent over the back of my legs. I feel one of his beefy hands grab hold of one ankle, tying it with rope, and then wraps the other ankle the same way. However, unlike my wrists, I can tell he has them wrapped tightly together. The bindings are so tight I can't even re-adjust either foot within the hold.

My whole body shudders; fear completely takes over as my mind runs through all the awful things this man could do to me. Spine-chilling images flash through my mind; from torture to sexual assault. The broken sob I release echoes around the cell.

A loud grunt behind me draws me back to the cell and his weight suddenly lifts off my rear. I try taking in a breath of relief but am quickly yanked back up to standing; Brute's hand digging into my arms hard enough to bruise.

Tears are pouring from my eyes, blurring the room. I jump out of my skin when the chair I was sitting in is kicked across the cell, splintering into pieces. Since my ankles are tied, I can't walk so Brute wraps the ropes from my hands around his and picks me up. He moves me back to the middle of the room before slamming my feet down on the ground. Pain shoots through my feet and legs causing me to cry out.

The resistance of the rope on my arms loosens a fraction as he takes each rope, one in each of his hands, and curls them around to my front. He picks up one end and tosses it to the right of our heads, before catching it, then yanking. My arm is immediately forced up and open above us. He keeps a tight hold of the end as he quickly does the same to the opposite rope until he has my arms spread wide like a 'Y' above us.

I stop looking at his hateful sneer long enough to tip my head back so I can see what is holding me up. Two large metal eyelets hang from the ceiling, dangling by metal chains. I trace the chain's tracks up and back as far as I can. It appears that the chains run through some kind of pulley system. Unfortunately, I can't turn my head enough to see what's behind me. *Although, maybe that's a good thing.*

Brute takes a step back and my head lolls forward, suddenly too heavy to hold up anymore. I have no idea how long it's been since I was taken but I know I haven't had anything to eat or drink since the guys' house. My strength is already withering away.

I didn't realize I closed my eyes, exhaustion kicking in due to adrenaline or maybe self-preservation, but they instantly snap open when I hear the clanking of chains behind me. Fear threatens to choke me as my arms slowly inch higher. Panic claws at my throat as I attempt to whip my legs around; trying and failing to kick out. I look down to discover that he has tied me to an eyelet on the floor in front of me. I'm literally unable to move anything except my head. After three more tugs, my feet are slightly raised off their heels, and I'm pulled tight enough to feel the burn in my shoulders.

Brute's footsteps are slow and methodical as he circles me, eyeing me like I'm his prey and he's the most horrifying damn predator in the world. After a whole lap around me, he stands in front of me and smirks like he's starving and I'm his next meal; and not in a sexy way.

Oh Hells Bells. I'm pretty sure the Devil himself chose this demon to walk Earth with us mere humans. His eyes are black and soulless as he sucks his teeth and cocks his head to the side.

His rough voice echoes around the cell, "Boss says you're special. *Are* you special? I don't see it. In fact, I don't know why he's bothering at all." He's not actually talking to me. He's just monologuing out loud, so I don't bother answering.

After a moment of deliberation, he hums out and continues. "Boss says he's got big plans for you. Congrats! You're going to be a Mom! But, shhhh, don't tell him. That can be our little secret, yeah?"

WHAT THE FUCK?! A broken sob rips from my soul as the images of me being assaulted repeatedly run through my mind. I don't think I can survive having that taken away from me, again. And

I *am* a Mom. *What the hell is Lukas getting at? If I tell him now that I can't have any more kids, will he believe me?*

Brute steps towards me, the smarmy grin on his face telling me he knows exactly where my mind went. "Don't worry, princess, everyone's been given strict orders to not go anywhere near your diseased snatch. No, you'll be a mom to our girls. You'll train them, make sure they're ready to go, and you'll be in charge of their health and wellbeing. No one likes sick or gangly merchandise, you see, so *your* job will be to make sure they're all ready and cared for before their new masters collect them."

The baritone in his voice is anything but comforting as my mind visualizes what he's saying. Lukas is going to force me to watch over the girls who are being trafficked. *Fuck that.*

"And if I say no?" I lift my chin defiantly, as high as I can, pushing through the pain and exhaustion.

Brute's eyes become hooded and his grin grows wider. "You say *no*, and *we* get to play, princess." He chuckles darkly as he walks behind me. I can hear him rummaging through things but can't place the sounds.

I flinch when he leans in, right behind me, and whispers in my ear, "And I do love to play." He punctuates his admission with a slice through the back of my shirt; nicking me in the process. I bite my lip to prevent crying out before another slice down my right arm strips me of that part of my shirt; leaving behind another trail of pain.

I hear him kneel down as he rubs my ass with his big meaty paws. I try to swing away from him but am reminded that my body is stretched tight with no give. He sniggers as he slices through my leggings on the right side. The cooler air hits my overheated skin and mixes with the pain from the cut. My body fires off so much adrenaline that I'm instantly dizzy.

"P-Please" I whimper. But he either doesn't hear or doesn't care. He makes his way to my left leg, grabbing a handful of my ass before ripping the knife down the side. He picks up momentum as he deftly slices down my left arm before ripping the pieces of my pants and shirt off of me, tossing them away. I'm left in the lacy blue bra and thong I wore to the guys house; however many days ago. My mouth fills with a familiar metallic taste, alerting me that I bit through the back of my lip in an effort to keep silent.

Shame and embarrassment fill my body. No one, other than my gynecologist, has seen this much of my body since having Josh. I don't even bother looking up at his eyes to see what he thinks. It won't make a difference. I let my head fall forward to my chest and close my eyes. But I can feel Brute standing in front of me, quietly assessing me.

Suddenly a hot, burning pain forces me to scream out. My eyes snap wide and I look down at some kind of brand searing into my chest over my right breast. The smell of burning flesh makes my stomach curl. I can feel urine running down my leg and just as I think I'm going to puke, he releases the brand from my chest. I watch with morbid fascination as the brand stretches some of the skin before leaving behind an angry design. Even though I am looking at it upside down, it looks like a thin triangle, pointed downwards, but open at the top like two doors opening wide. Like, a large thorn that's opened at the top.

My whole body trembles in pain, in fear, in shame. Snot and tears run down my face and I already feel like I can't survive this. I look back at Brute and watch as his smile grows as he tosses the brand aside, then slides a scalpel out of his pocket. "Oh, princess, we're just getting started." His eyes twinkle with a promise of gruesome things to come. *I can't do this. I won't survive.*

Just then, I recall my super power. I close my eyes and begin taking deep, settling breaths, like I learned so long ago. Mentally placing pain, embarrassment, and fear inside plastic boxes, taping them up, throwing them in a vault, locking it, then burying it under a whole truck of concrete.

I can vaguely see Brute's movements but it doesn't register; not really. Blood splatter grows across his face, shirt, the cell. But my brain doesn't process or feel any of it as I let my mind wrap me up in a dense fog and start to float. I release another deep breath, turn around in my mind, and jump into an endless pit of nothingness; delighted to arrive in a memory of my kids and I sharing dinner with my mother.

And there, I stay.

13

Cory

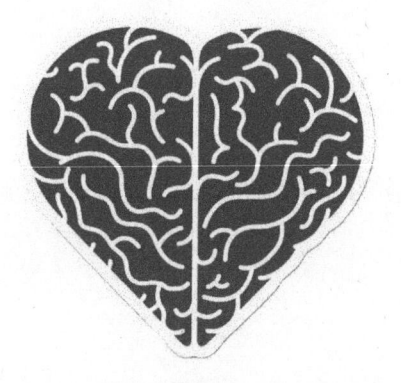

Order, predictability, control. Those are the things I need to survive. The guys work hard to balance me out but nothing they do can help me right now.

I've already re-organized every cabinet in the kitchen, scrubbed the bathrooms, and cleaned every mirror and window in the house. Now, I'm rearranging the library; sorting each genre alphabetically and placing them on separate bookshelves.

Our library is my favorite place in the entire house. The wall to the left boasts a custom made, built-in bookshelf stretching 21 feet wide and standing 9 feet tall. The outside and all the shelving is a dark cherry wood, perfectly polished at least every three months, by yours truly. The bookshelf consists of 6 extra wide segmented bookcases with 7 shelves each. The 7th segment is also extra wide but only has 5 spaced out shelves; for taller books.

The wall on the opposite end of the room is a giant window, overlooking the little oasis we built in the backyard. The long wall on the right has two more custom-made, built-in bookshelves, as tall as the other wall. That side only has 2 extra wide units because they sit on each side of a massive fireplace. It was the one thing Jenson insisted on.

He always wanted a fireplace, even though it rarely gets cold here. But, his mama had been more interested in drugs, and letting shitty men knock him around, than she was working and paying bills. Because of that, he spent a few winters cold with sometimes nothing more than a sheet to keep him warm.

Since it was so important to him, we also let him design it. He chose a gray and white stone design that reaches all the way to the ceiling and can heat the entire room in less than three minutes if needed.

There are couches, and a few large reading chairs sprinkled through the room, including a chaise lounge up next to the window. I can't help but picture Annie relaxing against the chaise, legs spread in front of her, nose in a book. We haven't talked much about it, but I know she's a reader. Hopefully she can find as much solace in this place as I have.

My vision blurs as tears begin to fill my eyes. I briskly swipe at my eyes while trying to clear my thoughts of the girl who consumes my every waking moment.

I force myself to return back to my task of taking the books out of each section, dusting them, cleaning them, then re-organizing. Not that there was anything wrong with how I had it. But, I figured moving the genres around the room would keep my mind busy.

The bluetooth speaker sitting on top of the mantle changes songs over. I'm just now starting on the fifth bookcase as the soothing voice of Teddy Swims flows through the room. I Lose Control has always been a good song to sing at the top of my lungs; just for fun. I could never really relate to it because, even with Amber, I had never had that kind of soul-owning experience. Like my entire being was owned by another and being separated from that person felt like it was ripping me apart; but that has definitely changed.

I start singing along while moving the suspense novels I transferred from the first case, onto their new shelves. I begin organizing them, alphabetically by author last name, in order of release; unless a series is disturbed.

This bookcase used to hold Jenson's smutty books, but I relocated those to the front. Don't ask why; I genuinely have no clue. And it definitely has nothing to do with the little platinum blonde vixen that has us wrapped around her finger. *The one who's missing.*

The second chorus rings out, striking painful chords deep in my heart. Impulsively, I start swiping the books off the shelves; sending them sailing across the floor. My hands are shaking violently and the words of the song settle deep into the marrow my bones. I crumble to the floor and gut-deep sobs wrack my body as I drown myself in tears. I'm such a mess without her; not knowing if she's ok or if I will ever see her again. If I will ever get to taste her sweet lips again, or hear the angelic sound of her laughter. If I will get to touch her porcelain skin or just sit back and bask in the light that shines through her.

I know Vince is out there looking for her. I *know* that in my head, but my heart says it's not enough. *I'm* not enough. I need to be doing something but I don't know what that something is. I feel like I'm failing her. My mind is in total disarray and can't give me order; can't give me steps to follow to make this right.

Footsteps alert me to someone approaching and I hastily try to gather myself; and the books I scattered on the floor. *That is definitely not how we treat books.*

My mental scolding does nothing to make me feel better.

An arm reaches out in my field of vision and begins picking up some of the books. We make our way across the floor until every book has been picked up and set down on the table so I can wipe them off properly.

We stand in silence for longer than feels comfortable. I don't even bother looking him in the eye; I can tell by the tattoos on his arms and hands who it is. Shame and embarrassment fills me as the silence stretches on. I see just enough of him that I watch as he shoves his hands into the pocket of his navy blue sweatpants, and rocks back on his heels like a kid.

Knowing his stubborn ass won't leave until I talk, I turn away from him, grab the wipes for the books, and begin cleaning them. As I begin setting them back on their shelves, I break the silence. "What's up?" I try to sound indifferent, but we both know it's bullshit. We've known each for far too long to hide.

"You tell me," he replies. I can hear him walk over to the plush black chair near the fireplace; the sounds of the fabric squishing beneath him as he sits. I turn to look over my shoulder to see him leaning back, fingers interlocked behind his head, head cocked and eyebrows raised.

I roll my eyes, shaking my head before turning back to my task. "Nothing. Just cleaning the bookshelves."

I hear his heavy exhale; silently calling me out.

For some reason, that sets me off. "What do you want me to say? That I feel like I'm drowning. That sitting around doing nothing is slowly killing me. That I spend every waking, and sleeping, moment consumed by thoughts of every moment we have spent with her and worrying we won't get more?" My voice is now bouncing off the walls around us. I feel my fists clenching as I stare at the books in front of me, willing them to soothe me, calm me.

But they don't. Instead, Jenson clears his throat and shifts in the chair before responding. "Dude, I know. I do. But you can't let that shit stay bottled up. You gotta talk to us, man."

"Why?" My voice breaks in agony. "Why would I when you're all feeling the same? I know you do. So why would I just add to it when we're all dealing with it?"

"*Because* we're all dealing with it!" His tone makes me flinch.

As his words sink in, I hang my head in shame, and suck in a deep breath. "I'm sorry. I know." I rub my hands over my face harshly before running them through my hair.

My next words came out just above a whisper because the sheer weight of them is too heavy to bear. "I've never felt like this. About a woman, I mean. I just miss her and I want to help find her. I *need* to help find her."

I finally turn to face him. He's now leaning forward in his chair, arms resting on his knees, head bent down, and hands running through his own hair. He nods a few times before raising his head to me. His eyes bore into mine, probing through my mind, my soul, for what feels like an eternity.

Suddenly, he claps his hands against his knees, rises to a stand, and says, "Well, let's go figure out how to help. Maybe we should find Nick. At this point, fuck waitin' around. There's got to be *something*."

And with that, he walks out of the library, leaving me to make the decision to follow or not.

Of course, I do.

14

Annie

Pain explodes from my knees and up my back, forcing me out of my dissociative state. I scream out in pain; or try to. My voice is dry and cracked from lack of water. By the time I remember where I am, who I'm with, I feel something that feels like leather wrap around my neck. I hear the click of metal behind my neck and feel whatever is attached to me pull high behind me and snap into place.

All at once, my pain receptors fire and I feel everything. I look down at my body, analyzing the bleeding cuts along my thighs and torso. My chest still only has the brand mark so, small miracles I guess.

Brute appears in front of me, clearly enjoying my pain, before unceremoniously jerking my arms in front of me. He swiftly binds my wrists together with thick, coarse rope. Once finished, he stands, eclipsing the dim light completely. He's lost the jacket since showing up here and blood splatter paints his black boots.

A waterfall of despair runs down my face. Before I can try to wipe it away, I'm yanked up under my arm. My knees quiver and threaten to buckle underneath my weight. It's at this point that I remember I'm only in my bra and panties. As Brute fiddles with something behind me, I mentally take stock of how *everything* feels. It doesn't feel like there was any penetration, which is a relief, but my back and legs feel like they've been slashed with a cat o' nine tails.

I hear something unclip and Brute walks in front of me, towards the cell door. He's holding onto some kind of leather band in his hand. Once he unlocks and opens the door, he looks back at me, impatience clear on his face. Before I can even voice a question, he yanks on the leather band and I stumble forward from the force placed on the back of my neck. *Oh my God! He put me in a collar and leashed me like a fucking dog!*

Images of the women on the boat flip through my mind as I take slow, timid steps towards him. I know better than to ask questions; he won't answer anyway. I try taking control of my breathing to keep calm but I can feel the oppressive weight of anxiety bearing down on me.

"Come on, Princess. We ain't got all day." Brute tugs on the leash, emphasizing his impatience. I urge my aching body to move faster as I take unsteady steps towards my certain demise. He waves for me to step in front of him, into the long, dim walkway.

We end up passing four cells, identical to mine, on the right side while the left is lined with exposed red brick. When I reach the end of the hall, my body shakes from exertion as I make my way up six concrete steps. I stare at the cold, metal door, fearing what horrors await me on the other side.

My body tenses as I feel Brute press against my back and slowly lean forward. His fist hammers out a tune and the door creaks on its hinges as it opens out into what looks like an underground bunker.

The space is ridiculously massive but I can't see everything from where I stand. What I can see shakes me to my very core. Cells, similar to the one I just left, line both walls. The middle of the room has 18 chains with big, rusty hooks hanging from the ceiling, spaced about 3 feet apart, placed in a circular pattern. They all hang down just enough that taller people, like Brute, can easily walk under them and reach them with ease.

What's inside the circle of hooks, has bile threatening to spill from my mouth. Two huge metal tables stand parallel to each other. They're each long enough to sit eight people but there's only three black metal folding chairs in the area. To the left of one table is a standing tool cabinet. Nothing special to look at, but the odd placement gives me an uneasy feeling.

Muffled cries, sobs, and whimpers pull me out of my perusal and I rapidly scan the cells on each side. Every cell, 14 in total, is occupied. Some have two or three women, young women, occupying them. Some barely look like they're 18 but none of them appear to be a day over 25. Every one of them is wearing what appears to be a baby doll chemise, but in different colors. Some women wear black, some red, and a lot are wearing white. I not-so-subtly scan each cell, each woman, trying to wrap my head around where I am and what the hell is going on.

Suddenly, one of the doors on my left clangs open and a young woman screams out in anger. I whip my head around, eyes widening as I take in the scene. A man with long, black hair and a rail thin frame is bending over the woman's cot, trying to get her up. She's kicking, thrashing, screaming, and clawing but he's not uttering a single sound. After maybe six or seven seconds, he lashes his hand out across her face, effectively silencing her.

The man jerks her up by her wrist and yanks her out of the cell, crossing over to the tool cabinet. She continues her struggle while I'm frozen in place; until Brute decides to shove me forward with a gruff command. "Move".

I flinch, having forgotten he was there, and move forward to the middle of the room. The large ceiling light above us casts the center of the room in blinding light but it isn't large enough to light up all of the cells. In this space though, I can see *everything*; *I wish I couldn't*.

I can see the bruises littering the woman's arms, face, and legs. The woman's eyes are wide, red-rimmed and glossy but her eyes are filled with fight and determination. Lanky man abruptly turns towards her, slapping a pair of metal cuffs around the wrist he currently has hold of. She lashes out at him, but he's faster. He grabs her arm mid-swing before closing the other end around that wrist.

Lanky Man fists the chain of the cuffs and drags her over to one of the hooks. She thrashes in his hold but it doesn't deter him. He quickly hoists her arms up and drops the chain of the cuffs over the hook. She drops down with an "oomph"; her shoulders taking the brunt of her weight as she dangles from the ceiling. Her toes are barely touching the floor but her persistence doesn't waver. She continues trying to kick and thrash out at her captor.

Seeming to have enough of her rebelliousness, the guy back hands her. She immediately falls silent; eyes fluttering closed and head rolling forward.

Brute's chortle of amusement sends shivers down my body as he pushes me forward. Lanky Man is rummaging through the cabinet by the time we step into the center of the room. He turns around, scans me from head to toe, and lifts his brow in question at Brute. Brute grunts, just grunts, and Lanky Man's mouth tips up in sick delight.

"Well, well, well, if it ain't her highness," He drawls condescendingly. He holds something from the cabinet in the palm of his hand as he stalks towards me. "Seems like today is training day for you."

His grin never falters; but mine is buried under a mound of pure terror. I stand there on shaky legs, staring into the black holes that have replaced his eyes.

He whips his hand out, grabbing hold of the collar around my neck with his fist, and forces me to meet his eyes. My toes scrape the floor, searching for purchase, and my lungs burn with the need to breathe.

"Boss man says you caused him a lot of trouble. Now you get to work off your crimes. Starting with her." He points to the unconscious woman behind him and my eyes widen even more.

"Wh-what do you mean?" My lips tremble in trepidation as I search the room for a way out; already knowing that search will be fruitless.

His cruel laughter rings out around the space that can only be described as a dungeon. "Well, sugar, you're in charge of making sure the girls follow directions, stay cleaned up and prepped for their new masters. If you fail, Brute's welcome will feel like child's play. If you succeed, your time here won't be filled with scars."

He clucks his tongue, tilts his head, and continues, "Well, not physical scars anyway."

He winks at me before turning back towards the woman hanging in the middle of the room. Waving something under her nose, she rouses back to consciousness. She starts struggling against the cuffs, tears streaming down her face as she attempts to get free.

Brute shoves me forward, causing me to stumble a couple of steps. I catch myself on the side of a table, and pause to catch my breath. Then, I weakly lift myself back into standing while eyeing the woman hanging in front of me.

Apparently, the woman didn't notice me while she was struggling with Lanky Man. But now she sees me; her eyes widen with hope and she starts screaming out for help.

I shake my head in disbelief, joining in her tears. "P-please. Don't.

Leave her alone!" I don't even know what I'm asking for but I can't, I *won't,* help them brainwash these women.

"Oh really?" Brute patronizes. I close my eyes knowing my outburst won't go unpunished. He steps in front of me and yanks me by my leash so I'm standing in front of the woman. "*You* convince her to calm down, or *you* take her place."

My breath stutters to a stop but I don't hesitate to answer. "Fine. Yes. I'll take her place. Just, please, leave her alone." Lanky Man chuckles like he knew exactly what I was going to say. *It's fine. I can handle it. Dissociation here I come.*

Brute tugs me over to a hook behind us, forcing me to face the other woman. Lanky man leans against one of the metal tables, arms folded across his chest, and a smile spreading across his face like he's a kid on Christmas morning.

"Lift your arms." Brute grunts out. I obey immediately as he bends down, lifting me up by my waist, and settling the coarse rope binding my wrists on the hook. He lets me go and my body drops a few inches. I groan out as my shoulders take the impact of my weight, and the various cuts littering my back and arms stretch.

My eyes have finally stopped flooding and I begin steadying my heart rate, preparing myself for what's to come. I slowly drown out my surroundings as the first whip of pain lashes across my stomach.

Before I can shut down completely, Lanky Man walks over and shoves his fingers deep in my throat. I cough and gag as drool spills out of my mouth. His cruel laughter fills the air as he grabs my ass with his other hand. "Oh, sugar." Lanky Man coos in my ear, "I've never understood the fat girl thing but seeing your tits and belly jiggle as he whips you has my dick so hard." He keeps thrusting his fingers in and out of my mouth like he's imagining it's his cock.

His eyes dilate with lust and he looks over my shoulder when he asks, "You think we can convince Boss Man to let us train her, too? May be fun?" He waggles his brows at Brute who strikes him in the shoulder with the whip. "Focus fucktard. Boss will tie you up by your intestines if you so much as touch her. And trust me, he'd hate to see what you're doing right now."

Lanky Man pouts and whines like someone took away his favorite toy. "But Brute, my cock's all hard now. What do I do about that?"

Brute lets out a grunt before peeling my head back by my hair, cutting off my ability to breathe. "Don't know. Don't care." I can feel him wrap my hair around his fist before swinging back for another swat. I slam my eyes closed as I struggle to breathe through the pain.

Lanky Man's footsteps have me opening my eyes again. I watch as he strolls over to the cabinet, pulls out a syringe with a bottle of something clear. He tips the bottle upside down, sticks the needle in, and draws in some of the liquid. I barely blink before he steps up to the woman and injects her in the side of the throat.

My mind tells me it's time to go into the void but the lack of oxygen is preventing me from transitioning. So, I'm forced to watch. I watch as the woman's arms go slack. I watch as her head slumps forward. And I watch as Lanky Man lifts her cuffed hands up and off the hook, dumping her over his shoulder.

He casually takes the seven steps over to the outside of the metal table, twists her so she's facing towards the center, and flops her on the table with a loud thump. I wince at the sound, knowing that will absolutely hurt. But, she doesn't make a sound, doesn't twitch; nothing.

Brute whips me two more times across my back before releasing my hair. I drop my head to my chest and start gulping in the air I so desperately need. He steps in front of me and grabs my jaw between his fingers, squeezing hard. "Now, be a good little Mom and watch what happens when your girls are disrespectful."

I go to close my eyes shut but he squeezes harder before gritting out. "If you don't watch, we will line up every damn girl in her until they have all received the same."

My eyes snap open and the promise of violence ripples from his eyes. I nod as much as I can until he steps back; just enough to let me watch Lanky Man maneuvering the young woman on the table. He twists her head so that she faces me. Her eyes are filled with terror as he positions her like she's a ragdoll.

"What did you do to her?" My question puffs out as a squeak and I'm shaking my head in disbelief. Lanky Man smiles up at me, lifting the girl's white chemise, revealing her bare ass. His stare penetrates mine and I see every disgusting intention.

"You like that, sugar? We have a special little cocktail just for our little toys who behave badly." His smile turns into an evil grin as his eyebrows raise in excitement. "You see, our little fighter here still has a lot to learn. It's our job to make her realize that she has a choice. She can either submit to us, and her future master, or we make her. The best part is," He leans in like he's sharing a juicy secret. "She can't move any part of her body, but she can still feel *everything*."

A loud slap on her ass cheek echoes around the room and he stares at her unmoving body; as if to prove his point. He shrugs his shoulders and chuckles as he unbuckles his belt. With a twist of his fingers, his button comes undone and the zipper opening sounds louder than a gunshot.

Realizing what he's about to do, I scream out, "Wait! I took her punishment! I did. You said you'd leave her alone!"

Lanky Man's answering laugh is sown right creepy as he simply states, "I changed my mind. Consider this lesson number 1."

I stop focusing on him; much to my horror, my mind already knows where this is going. I look at the woman lying helplessly on the table and an entire conversation passes between us. I want so desperately to dissociate. *Now's the perfect time.* But, I can't bring myself to do it. She doesn't want to be alone. She doesn't need to be alone.

I inhale deeply and stare into her eyes, nodding at her once to show I'm here. Even though it may not help at all, I'm still here. Her eyes slowly transition from terror to resolve.

The metal table grinds against the floor as her body is pushed forward. Tears continue to stream down her nose, dropping to the table, but her eyes never wander from mine.

We spend the rest of our time in the room having silent conversations about nothing important; cementing our bond to each other. One forged in pain and trauma.

15

Nick- One week later

Annie's been gone for almost two weeks now, and we're no closer to finding her. My programs have been running facial recognition on every damn security camera, public or private, that I could hack into. I'm losing sense of time. I sleep for a few hours, go for a run to clear my head, then head to the office. We still need to roll out the programs for the youth center but, other than that, I spend every waking moment searching for Annie.

Cory and Jenson decided a few days ago to meet up with Lana and make flyers asking for information on Annie. But, so far, all the tips have been dead ends; each one killing off another piece of my soul.

Anger and rage are slowly taking over me and I'm having a hard time masking them. I'm moments from combusting and I just know that when it happens, I won't be able to find my way back.

I'm leaning back in my desk chair, flipping my blade across my knuckles absentmindedly. I have done it so many times over the years it's as easy as breathing air. Not to brag but, my skill with my blades is pretty fucking fantastic, too. Not only do I have steady hands for executing the most perfect of slices, but I can hit a bullseye from 30 feet away. Any further and I can hit my target, but not dead on.

I smile as I think about Vince's face when he first saw me throw. We were at his Dad's range and had the whole place to ourselves. His brows disappeared into his hairline and his eyes bulged in shock after I hit ten targets perfectly. I'm still shit with a gun but, I can't deny how amazing it felt having him press up against me, trying to perfect my form.

That was a few months before I got drunk and blurted out my feelings. Years of being best friends with the only man I have ever loved was the sweetest kind of torture. I scoff at myself when I remember the stupid grin on his face after I told him how much I wanted him. As usual, Vince knew exactly what was happening in my brain because the moment I started spiraling in shame and embarrassment, he grabbed me by the back of my neck and mashed his lips to mine. My fingers reach up to touch my lips as the phantom feeling from the past graces my lips.

Then, the memory transforms into another. One where Vince opened up about his past, right before we all decided to buy this place. He wanted to make sure we all knew what we were getting into. While we were all shocked about his Dad's ties with a gang in Chicago, none of us were willing to walk away from our friendship due his Dad's past.

Suddenly, an idea hits me. Before I bother talking myself out of it, I send a message to Vince to call me as soon as he can. A loose plan is already forming in my mind but I fight the urge to bring Cory and Jense into it. First, I need to talk to Vince. Then, we get our fucking girl back.

Six hours later, I'm back at home and making a rough outline of my plan. Vince hesitantly agreed with our plan, letting me know just how far this has pushed him. He's always been one to walk the straight and narrow; always encouraging us to do the same. He isn't a dirty cop or running anything nefarious in the background. He's genuinely a stand-up guy, and a hero.

Unfortunately, not being able to find Annie is pushing him past his breaking point. We're all a mess. We almost never eat together, rarely talk about anything other than surface-level bullshit, and we're all circling the drain. Each new morning reminds us of another day she isn't with us, and depression has us all by the throats. But hopefully, that will all change tonight.

Leo's metal cover of Heathens blares from the speakers on my computer as I cast a wider net for facial identification. Since hanging up with Vince, I've been filled with a stronger resolve. I *know* this can work, we just need to get the ball rolling; like yesterday.

A notification on my screen alerts me that someone has deactivated our house alarm. I click over and see that Vince is walking in, carrying a ridiculous amount of pizza. The first genuine smile I have felt in the last two weeks stretches across my face as I click the music program closed and jog out of my room.

I feel a sense of excitement as I trot down the steps before jumping the last three; landing with a thud in front of Vince. He startles in surprise before looking at me like I've lost my mind. Maybe I have but the smile on my face feels amazing so, whatever.

He sets the pizzas down on the foyer table before turning to me. I step into him before he can react and mold my lips to his, pouring all of my hope and love into it. After a beat, he recovers from his surprise and fists my shirt, pulling me in even closer and kissing me; matching my enthusiasm.

We break apart, only to catch our breaths, and spend a moment soaking in the little bubble we're currently in. His eyes soften from intense to loving as he leans his forehead against mine, and inhales deeply. My eyes close and I melt into his touch.

The turning of the door knob breaks our trance and we step back, giving each other one last lingering look. We face the door in time to see Cory and Jenson walk in. They each hang their keys on their personalized key holders by the door and step closer to us. Jenson cracks a tiny grin before asking, "So, are we going to eat pizza in the foyer or..." He trails off and cocks his brow playfully.

Vince picks up the pizzas and nods his head towards the kitchen, silently commanding us to follow. He strolls into the kitchen and sets the pizzas on the table. Cory veers off towards the island, pulling out beers from our beer fridge, and takes them to the table. Jenson pulls out plates and I grab the napkins. We all make our plates, take our seats, and silently enjoy the first meal we've had together in a week.

After his first plate is cleared, Cory makes himself another before clearing his throat and breaking the silence, "Alright boys, what did we need to meet about? I know it's not good news/bad news with Annie because the air is all wrong. So, spill it."

Vince and I look at each other, reaffirming that we both agree this could work. With a subtle nod, we turn our glances back to Cory and Jense. Vince swallows the mouth full he has, takes a swig of beer, and leans forward; resting his arms on the table. "I'm thinking about having a talk with my dad. *If* I do that, *and* he agrees, I want to try and contact the man he handed his gang over to. *If* it's still up and running, they'll have a lot more power, and people, than the PD and the fucking Black Thorns combined." He spits out the Black Thorns like he's cursing it.

The kitchen is silent for a long time as Cory and Jenson digest what Vince is saying, and what this could mean in terms of finding Annie. They both look at each other and a silent conversation passes between them.

When they turn back to face us, Vince holds up his hand to stop them. "Before you decide anything, you *do not* have to be involved in this. If this happens, it will be dangerous and it will *not* be legal. I'll most likely lose my job but I don't even care about that right now. I just want Annie back. You do not have to be involved in any way. I just wanted to let you know what I'm considering. Nick called me about it earlier, and," he sighs heavily, rubbing his hands over his face before finishing his thought. "I think this is the fastest option, with the best outcome. Lukas' gang is so tied into the underground, local PD can't catch up with them fast enough. I'm afraid if we don't do this, we're going to lose her forever." His voice catches at the end and his eyes glisten with unshed tears.

Cory and Jenson raise their brows in question at him before Jenson responds. "Dude, we're in. We're all in. Period. We've all stayed pretty above board with our dealings but, I agree. If there's a chance we can get help, we should take it. I also want to be involved when we go in to get her." He pauses to look at Cory and turns back to Vince, "We both do."

Vince exhales deeply before nodding his head in agreement. We spend the rest of dinner planning our next moves. Excitement fills the air as the possibility of getting to Annie increases. *Now we just have to convince his dad to give up his old contact.*

16

Annie

I'm not sure how long it's been since I was taken, but I'm definitely pissing people off. Since the first day in "the training room", as the douche canoes who run this place call it, there's been a decent schedule that helps me sort of keep track of time. Based on the schedule, I think my first official training day was 8 or 9 days ago. And it has been a very fucked up 8 or 9 days.

After the welcoming from hell, and the time I spent locked in a silent world with Jodie, Brute uncuffed me before tossing Jodie and I into the cell she was staying in. It had two small cots, each with a thin navy sheet. There was a bucket that sits in the corner for bathroom needs and a roll of cheap ass toilet paper.

Before he closed the door, he reminded me that I needed to take care of her wounds and, if she wanted to, she could help me with mine. He tossed in a medium-sized first aid kit before slamming the door shut and locking it. Jodie had already climbed onto her cot, facing the left wall. Another loud door was slammed; echoing through the silence.

After a brief moment, a female's voice shouted, "Clear", before hushed whispers filtered through the space. I didn't pay them any mind; not yet. Instead, I crawled over to the kit, groaning in pain as the cuts and lashes stretched with the movement. Then I slowly make my way towards Jodie.

When I finally get to her cot, I hear her muffled whimpers and choked sobs. I don't want to startle her, and I definitely don't want to touch her without her permission.

Since she's facing the wall, I know she can't see me. I choose to just sit here quietly with my lower back leaning on the side of her cot. The longer I sit there, staring at the drain in the middle of the floor, the more completely hopeless I feel. *I asked him for the punishment. So why? Why did he rape her? What the hell was the point?*

I waited for a few minutes before whispering the only thing I could even think to say, "I'm so sorry. I'm so, so sorry." Then, the dam breaks and I join her in letting the emotions flow from our eyes.

Eventually, she turns over, and tenderly places her hand on my shoulder, squeezing slightly. I reach up and squeeze hers in return.

After another minute in silence, she allows me to clean up her wounds. I gingerly clean the angry marks around her wrist from the cuffs. Then I work on the split on her cheek from one of the slaps.

I saved the worst for last. I wanted to give her as much kindness and care as possible before asking if I could check her vaginal area.

With tears in her eyes, she nods before lying back and allowing me to clean and stitch up her perineal tear.

Once I was finished checking her over, she started cleaning up the wounds I've collected since being taken. It was then we told each other our names, and she told me a little bit about her life before this.

Since that day, I've had to spend time with each girl; cleaning them, their clothes, their bathroom buckets. I'm supposed to calm them, convince them to stay quiet, no matter the consequence, and teach them Lukas' rules for inspection time. Thoughts of my kids frequently fill my mind, helping to blot out the overwhelming sense of despondency. I try to treat each young woman like they're my own.

It didn't take long to notice the ones in red and black chemises don't make eye contact with me and have definitely been here longer; or they've at least learned how to play the game. The ones in white are more talkative and definitely struggle the most with being here. Regardless, I try to treat them all with respect and care, hoping they understand that I may not be "for sale" like they are, but I don't want this any more than they do.

The good news is, Lukas hasn't talked to me, other than a very brief conversation four days ago. He explained his expectations, as well as the punishments if I fail. He legitimately looked in my eyes, like this was a business meeting, and said, "Our goal is to train them to be perfectly submissive for their new masters. That's what we get paid for."

I scoffed and rolled my eyes before stupidly blurting out, "I think you need to look up BDSM etiquette. Pretty sure consent is one of the core principles, so stop using the terminology trying to make it sound like anything other than rape and human trafficking. Call a spade, a spade." For some reason, he actually let me finish that thought before he flew over the table, grabbed the back of my head, and bashed my head down.

While that *should* have taught me a lesson, I actually got in trouble shortly after. I didn't even mean to; not like when I sassed Lukas. But, without my meds, I'm having a hard time controlling my emotions, staying present, and focusing on starting, and finishing, any single task. And what happened *two* days ago, well I'll chalk that up to duress; or maybe a psychotic break.

The douche crew comes walking through, flinging sandwiches and miniature bottles of water into our cells before walking right back out the door. *Pricks.* It briefly pulls me from my mind as I go to retrieve our lunch. I shuffle to Jodie, placing hers near her chest so she doesn't have to move much to get it. She's still healing and has already ripped her stitches once.

She sends me a gentle smile in thanks and I nod at her before making my way back to my cot. I groan as I sit criss-cross in the middle, leaning my back against the wall. Then, I basically inhale the sandwich since I lost my food privileges for the last 6 meals. They said I didn't deserve it because I had "interfered with a training session." *What-the fuck-ever.*

I was busy washing the basically see-through chemises in a giant steel vat on wheels. Every day they roll it in and I'm escorted from my cell to the far left corner to wash clothes. I usually did this quickly and as quietly as possible. *I mean, come on, I'm not about to get hit for dirty laundry.*

But, on that day, the woman they were training, Camila, had been in table pose for *a whole hour* while The Fucktard Twins sat back, ate their breakfast, and talked about sports. Those two are the worst. They're scum that act like big shots but probably don't have a fully functioning brain between them.

After they finished stuffing their ugly faces, they decided to clean the tools in the cabinets. Once cleaned, they placed them on her back then swatted her ass each time. I could see her biting her lip to prevent from crying out.

My right eye started twitching as I watched her arms tremble and then, they upped their assholery. They took turns repeatedly spanking her, yanking her head back, spitting on her. And all the while she managed to keep table pose. I guess Fucktard One was determined to see her fall, so he kicked her in the stomach, causing her to crash face-first into the concrete; the tools clanking to the ground around her.

They had the audacity to become irate, like it wasn't *their* fault she fucking fell! Fucktard One started screaming about her being a "shitty whore". Then he pulled her up by her hair and threw her over the metal table. Her screams echoed around the dungeon and they chortled in amusement; like this was their plan all along.

Fucktard Two picked her up by her neck, slamming her down on the table as he ripped the chemise off her body. He snarled out, loud enough for everyone to hear, "If you can't follow simple directions, maybe we can at least teach you how to take two cocks."

Somewhere in the back of my mind, I could hear her screams mingle with their laughter as they pawed at her body. But, I couldn't see it.

I just. Saw. Red.

It descended over my eyes like a red haze was falling from the sky.

As the haze settled, it felt like someone took over my body with no way to stop it. I was suddenly bashing Fucktard Two in the back of the head with whatever tool I had scooped up on my way; the pile that fell with her was still scattered on the floor. The crunch of bones and an anguished scream vaguely reach my ears. Not that it registered at the time; or mattered. I had already jumped on Fucktard One, and was hitting him repeatedly.

I'm not sure how many times I hit him, or who pulled me off of him, but I vaguely registered that Camila had at least made it back to the safety of her cell.

The red haze that had settled over me was cast out the moment my head was submerged in ice cold water. I quickly realized that there was a hand on the back of my neck and another was holding both of my wrists behind me. The man's body draped over mine, making sure I couldn't move or lift my head up. He dunked me four times; each time feeling like I was under longer.

When he decided I had enough, he dragged me by my hair back to the mini-dungeon, while I coughed, spit, and gasped for breath. After he threw me back in the single cell, I looked up in time to see Brute's terrifying face and murderous stare. He slammed the door, locked it, then walked away. I greedily gulped in air as I waited for the sound of the second door closing. But, before it came, the lights went out and I was plunged into darkness. The second door slammed shut and I was finally alone.

Exhaustion weighed heavily on me as I curled up in the corner. My mind wanted to relive what had just happened but I pushed it away. Just for now.

As soon as I got my breathing under control, I began opening the void in my mind. My kids are there, laughing with my mom. My guys are there, too. Even if I never see them again, I still get to live in the memories we shared. So, in that moment, I was thankful for the time to see them, to feel them. Even if it was all in my head.

A door banging open startles me out of the memories of the last few days. I shake my head, ridding it of the hundreds of images flashing through my mind like a macabre film.

I haven't intervened with anyone else; not like that. But, then again, she was only the second one they tried raping in front of me. *Should I have done more to intervene during the other physical elements? Am I helping or hurting?*

I feel wetness pooling in my cleavage and my little ADHD brain unhelpfully supplies the tune of Tears Don't Fall by Bullet for My Valentine. Of course, this sparks a maniacal mix of laughter and bawling. A brief glance shows that Jodie is looking at me from her cot, a mixture of fear and concern swirling in her eyes.

"Oh Sugar, did we break you already?" Lanky Man's slimy voice rises just above my own hysteria. I look over at him, leaning up against the bars, smug as ever. I take him in as I try to clear the tears from my eyes. He's standing there like he's hot shit when really he's just one of Lukas' lap dogs.

A visual from a TikTok I saw plays in my head. It was a video of a Great Dane jumping on a rocking recliner and tipping it over. But, in my head, Lanky Man's face was on the Great Dane's body.

Naturally, I burst out laughing again.

This time, tears stream down my face from hysteria instead of guilt. I'm suddenly bending over, head between my legs wrapping my arms around my stomach trying to hold myself together.

I peer over at Lanky Man, and see his face twisted in confusion. He looks like someone told a simple joke but it went straight over his head, further making him look like an idiot.

I can't help it. I laugh harder.

I vaguely hear him murmur something about "crazy bitches" before he unlocks the cell and makes his way to me; his face now twisted in anger. He reaches down and pulls me up by my bicep; fingers digging into the muscle.

He puts his other hand around my other arm and pulls me up until we are nose-to-nose. I widen my eyes at the proximity, my laughter and tears coming to an abrupt stop. He sneers in my face and spits out, "The fuck is wrong with you stupid bitch? Maybe you need to be taught a lesson on laughing out of turn." *Huh? How does that even make sense?*

So, um, I apparently stay on the crazy train and start laughing again.

Apparently, that wasn't the correct response because he roars in my face; his breath smelling like limburger cheese. *Gag.* The he whips me around, my back to his chest, twisting my arms behind my back and marching me out of the cell. I cough back my laughter and tears, trying *really* hard to get a grip.

It's not until I see one of the tables laid out with different burning elements that I regain my sanity; or what's left of it. Adrenaline spikes through my system as fear takes the place of humor. I'm hit in the back of the head by something hard enough to rattle my noggin and prevent me from reacting to his next moves. My hands are cuffed, the metal biting into the bone through my skin, and I'm quickly hoisted onto a hook.

Just as I start clearing my head from the hit, the hook starts moving and I'm lifting in the air. "What the fuck!" I screech.

In seconds, I'm completely lifted off of my feet and no amount of moving helps me touch the floor. My shoulders are screaming and I'm already having a hard time breathing. Lanky Man's cruel laughter rings out around the room and I refocus on him moving across the room; coming to a stop in front of me.

My breathing is heavy and my heart is pounding in my ears and I see the glint of something shining from his hand as he moves closer. It's then I realize that this next part is *really* going to suck. I clench my jaw and stare directly into his eyes, steadying my breathing as he moves closer.

"You hurt my friends, Cunt. And for *that*, you will pay." His low raspy voice is punctuated with a sharp pain across my lower belly. Tears prick my eyes and I bite my inner-cheek to prevent myself from screaming. His sneer tells me he's nowhere near done so I begin to take deep, slow breaths, and find the nothingness in my mind.

This time, it brings me to the last night I spent with the guys. After me sharing my past, after the tears, after the most amazing heart-melting kisses. Just us, watching tv on the couch and enjoying each other's company. And I let myself stay in that memory as long as I can.

17

Jenson

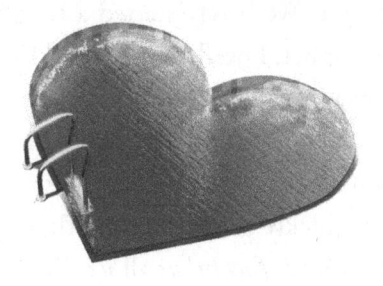

We're getting close to the neighborhood where Vince's dad, Wes, lives. Last night, Vince asked if we could come by in the morning. He gave his usual 'dad' guilt speech, laughing as Vince and I groaned. But, we agreed to bringing him breakfast and catching up *before* we talk about anything serious.

I love Vince's old man. He took me in when he didn't need to. Didn't even try going the legal route, didn't care about the money he would be out or anything. In fact, he spoiled me before I moved in. I think he knew what was happening with my Mom's long line of "suitors".

Once I woke up in the hospital, alone, I made the decision to leave. Mom not only let that son of a bitch damn near beat me to death but she didn't even bother coming to visit. When I was discharged, Vince and Wes were there to pack me up and take me home. The rest is history. I would do anything for this man. *Single Dad of the century!*

The radio has been turned down low enough for us to talk over and prepare for what we are going to do over the next few days. We've already decided that we're taking a whole damn week off. We're done waiting. Whatever needs to happen to find her, we're going to do it.

As we make a left turn on his street, we're all talked out; needing this next piece before doing any more planning. It's then that I hear the song on the radio. Beautiful Crazy by Luke Combs softly plays in the cab and my whole body tenses. The lyrics call me and all my ridiculous feelings out. We barely started a relationship and I'm already head over ass for her. I need her back and I know my soul won't heal until that happens.

A sniff coming from the front seat has me leaning forward a bit from my spot behind Vince. Nick swipes at his face and turns to look out the window. I quickly glance at the other two and realization dawns on me. *This song is fuckin' us* all *up.* I'm not sure why but, it actually gives me peace knowing that she doesn't just have one or even two of us falling for her; she has all four of us.

We pull into the driveway and Wes is already sitting on his porch swing, coffee in hand. I can hear the collective breath we all take before slapping on our best fake smiles. Not fake, fake, but not truly happy right now, either.

As we climb from the truck, Wes comes walking over and wraps his arms around Vince, giving him a big slap on the back, before making his way to the rest of us. Honestly, this man is the only real parent between the four of us and bless him for taking in all of our raggedy asses.

It's always crazy to see him and Vince next to one another. You would almost think they're brothers. They're the same height, have big, bulky muscles, brown eyes and a smile that makes you feel like you're truly important and cared for.

I smile up at him as he waves for us to follow him through the front door. His house has a suburban cottage charm which is completely opposite of what he looks like, but he makes it work.

We follow him through the front door, making sure to take off our shoes on the mat to the right. He is pretty particular about his oak floors and the man loves neutral tones. The dining room fills the space immediately to our left; a simple dark wooden table with 6 matching chairs sits in the center of the room. Underneath is this massive beige rug that has gray geometric patterns swirling around it.

The wall perpendicular to the open space of the foyer has an arched entrance leading to the kitchen; which leads right through to the living room. But, as usual, we never make it that far.

Vince unpacks the doughnuts and kolaches we bought on the way here, we take turns pouring coffee, and take our spots around the island while chatting. I'm not even sure why but we have always gravitated to this area. It's not necessarily big, there's no room for stools, and it's barely large enough for all five of us to stand around it but, it's been this way since we were teens.

We spend the next twenty minutes catching up, laughing about the blind date one of his neighbors set him up with, and explaining our new venture with the youth center. Seeing that man beam with pride at all of us definitely checked a lot of "little boy me" boxes.

Once there was a lull in the conversation, Wes gives us each "the look". You know the one. Then, he refreshes his coffee and moves to the living room. Claiming his huge black recliner, he exhales heavily, and waits silently for us to follow. *I swear this man is a mind reader.*

We all follow behind, Vince and Nick sitting on the loveseat to the left of his dad and Cory and I sitting on the couch across from them. We all look at one another, wondering if he's going to flip shit or deny us all together but, with a nod, we move forward.

Vince clears his throat and turns to his dad. "So, I know that we haven't talked a lot about our life before moving here." Wes hums and eyes him warily, clearly disliking where this is going.

Sensing his dad's discomfort, Vince spews it all out in one breath. "Annie was taken two weeks ago by a shitty ex who leads a local gang. It's taking way too long to find her, we've run out of leads and we're officially desperate. She has kids, Dad. Kids that need her. Her mom has them, right now, but this is killing her, too. I, well, we wanted to talk to you today because we're hoping you'll give us the name of one of your contacts with the gang you used to run. I'm hoping I can convince them to join forces with us and help us get our girl back." Vince sucks in a deep breath before adding one final plea, "Dad, please, we have to find her."

The room descends in absolute silence. Nothing but the pounding in my ears makes a noise and we all hold a collective breath. Wes doesn't move, doesn't speak. He just looks at each of us, searching for the answer to a question we don't even know.

After a whole ass eternity, ok maybe just like three minutes, he sits forward, and rests his arms on his knees. He stares into Vince's eyes before tilting his head. With a subtle nods, he takes a deep breath and pushes it out. Scrubbing his hands up and down his face, he finally settles back and delivers his verdict. "Son, I know Annie means a lot to you. I do. But all of you have worked so damn hard to get where you are. None of you had easy upbringings but you didn't stray from your paths. You got shit done, made yourself into men, good men, and you did it with no one's help. That's not something to just throw away."

Disappointment and despair spear through my heart and I have to consciously focus on breathing through it. But, he's right we have no connections other than the PD and we're still no closer to finding Annie. This was our only option.

Just as I begin losing myself, he huffs out a deep sigh and says, "Once you do this, you can't go back, son. Any of you."

He looks at each of us in turn before continuing. "I don't know how Enzo runs things but we do talk occasionally. Nothing business or too personal and always on a burner phone. I moved fire and brimstone to get us out, son. After your mom died, I just couldn't do it anymore. I didn't want you to grow up with a bitter, angry man and I knew my heart would harden the longer I stayed. Just remember, this isn't kiddie stuff; it's not a game."

Cory begins to interject but Wes holds his hand up to pause him. "But, I know you all know that. I've seen you all train, I've seen you all reveling in the power of escape out at the range, but this is real life. You've all had your own versions of monsters but what you're thinking about getting mixed up in," He shakes his head for a moment then lowers his voice. "These aren't monsters. These are demons from the pits of hell. They aren't friends, or drinking buddies. You cross them, sometimes even verbally, and you'll end up with a bullet in your skull; *if* you're lucky."

He leaves us to deal with our own thoughts and emotions for a couple of minutes before leaning forward. "Are you ready to give up your career, your life, to find this woman?" Not a single second passes by before we all say, "Yes."

He lets a few beats pass until his lips turn up into a grin, "Well boys, I never wanted this for you, but I know you can all handle it. And, I'm happy for you all. I look forward to meeting this very special woman once all of this is over. Until then, I'll help in any way I can but keep in mind, this old man is not cut out for field work any more." He pairs his statement with a chuckle and slaps at his belly like he isn't still rockin' a six-pack.

We all grin and roll our eyes but give our silent agreement. We're in. All in. And now we're that much closer to finding our girl.

Vince hops up, pulls his dad up to a stand, and wraps him in the tightest hug I have ever seen. Wes lets out a grunt but manages to pat

Vince's back in the way dads do. Once they break apart, we all join in and laugh as the old man pretends to preen at the attention.

Stepping back, we all take a deep breath before Wes tells us to follow him as he heads to his office. *Hell yes. Let's do this!*

18

Cory

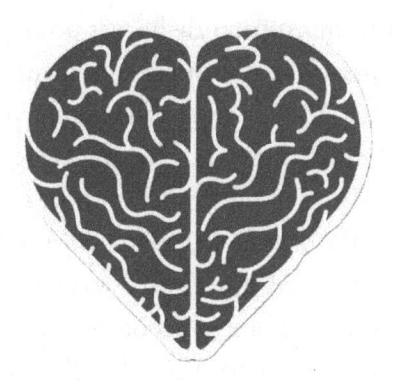

The last 36 hours have been a whirlwind of planning; and more planning. It's my favorite thing ever and I *finally* feel like I'm doing something productive. We've left the gym in the hands of our three most trusted employees. Because of that, coupled with Nick's security systems accessible on our phones, we can put it out of our mind for a little while.

When we first piled into Wes' office, he unlocked the bottom drawer of his desk, hit some keys that made beeping sounds, and opened a lid. I was on the other side of the desk so I can only assume it was a small safe. He pulled out a shitty ass burner phone and dialed a number, then left some coded message about vacations in California and hung up.

We all just stared at him as he booted up his computer and stuck a flash drive he also retrieved from the lock box. None of us said anything because, well, what would we say?

After a few moments typing away, he clicked open a folder and turned the laptop towards us. My first thought was, *Holy shit*. My next thought was, *We seriously thought he was in a low-level, jacking around gang. We were so very wrong.*

He spent the next forty-five minutes giving us a run-down of the major players he used to deal with and pointing out people to stay far the fuck away from. Apparently he was powerful enough that he made enemies. I mean, he did move and change their names but, damn. He also asked Nick to set up an encrypted email so he could send us some "helpful documents." We quickly realized this man had dirt- lifetime behind bars or buried 6-feet under kind of dirt- on hundreds of men. Even the ones he was friends with and was loyal to.

At one point, I noticed Vince's face was a mix between a frown and confusion. None of us are saints but we aren't criminals, either. Vince, though, his whole life has been about protecting our community. The mental war going on in his head must be killing him; so I made a note to bring it up when we get home.

As we continued going through the information about dealings, and people, and all the other shit this man used to be wrapped up in, I finally blurted out the question that had been burning in my mind since he connected the flash drive. "Why do you still have all of this if you got out?" I glanced at the others, and noticed them all raise their brows in curiosity, too.

Wes' whole face changed. An evil smirk curled his lips as he cocked a brow, leaned back in his chair, and shrugged before stating, "Insurance." That was it. No explanation; no nothing. But, I won't lie, it sent a shiver down my back. *We definitely don't know this side of Wes.*

A man named Enzo called while we were still shifting through documents to try to find multiple people we can ask for help, if needed. Wes told Enzo he needed favor and Enzo was far too damn happy to oblige. Wes put Enzo on speakerphone before nodding at Vince to make our case with as few incriminating descriptors as possible.

Imagine our surprise when Enzo cursed in outrage over hearing that the Black Thorns were responsible for our current grief. Apparently, they had been screwing with the shipments coming in through the bay and it was costing Enzo greatly.

The phone call lasted maybe two minutes. Before he hung up, he told us he'd have a plane ready for us at noon today so we could go meet him in person. He was all too willing to help Wes. Apparently Wes had saved this man's life repeatedly, but the nail in the coffin to help was hearing that the Black Thorns were involved.

Now, we're sitting on a fucking private jet, going over plans, hopes, ideas, everything. I keep fiddling with the hem of my shirt, wiping my hands down my pants, and twirling my pen in the air. I have so much pent up energy and excitement but it has nowhere to go. It's not like there's a row machine or treadmill on this plane.

After five more minutes, I've successfully irritated myself. I unbuckle my belt and stride to the bar counter. Pouring two fingers of whiskey, I throw it back before pouring another. Walking to the back where the bed is, I place my bag on the bed. It's been a while since I sketched anything but I really need something to concentrate on to release this energy. I tried reading, but after every other sentence I would stall out with thoughts of Annie.

I pull out my new packages of Faber-Castell Pitt Graphite Pencils and sketch pad. Flipping open to a new page, I lie on my stomach on the bed and let it all out.

The feeling of the graphite scratching against the paper lowers my anxiety. The sounds of the pencil gliding across the paper quiets the noises in my head. I can physically feel the tension leaving my body, the worst-case scenarios playing in my head dim down before disappearing completely; until I'm just me. At this moment, I'm merely existing and allowing my subconscious to take over and drive for a bit.

And I. Just. Drift.

A knock on the door startles me and I whip my head around, taking in my surroundings. It takes me a moment but I finally remember we're on a plane to meet Enzo. I shake my head to re-awaken my body.

When my brain catches up, I rattle out a hoarse, "Come in." I clear my throat as I hear the door open behind me. Turning my head, I see Jense standing in the door frame, hands spread out on both sides, leaning forward into the room.

His lips tip up in a gentle smile before saying, "Hey. Sorry, you were in here for the rest of the trip. We're about to land so we have to get the seat belts back on." He nods his head behind him, gesturing for me to follow, before turning around and walking back.

I can feel my cheeks heat up thinking about how his arms and chest looked defined through his shirt as he leaned in the room; stretching the fabric across his body. *Jesus Cory. That was one fucking time years ago and we both agreed too much booze was involved and we'd pretend it didn't happen.*

I scoff at my own stupidity because I sure as hell have never forgotten about feeling his stubble against my body as he traveled down my... *Nope. Snap out of it. You've done so good hiding this ridiculous crush. Annie. Focus on Annie.*

I bet it's just hormones or emotions or something since she's missing. *Yeah right.*

I slowly scoot off the bed, trying to will my now aching cock to go away. My muscles are stiff so I try to stretch them out, as I stand with a groan.

If we're landing, that means I have been sketching on that bed for over an hour. But, I'm sure as hell not going to complain. I feel so much lighter than I did when I came in here and I can finally focus solely on Annie.

I flip my sketchbook closed, not even bothering to look at whatever contorted bullshit I drew, and pack up my supplies. Once I leave the room, I head back to my seat and buckle in just as the plane begins its descent.

I lean my head back, closing my eyes, a smile playing on my mouth as I think about how much closer we are to finding Annie.

Jenson bumps my elbow with his, causing me to look over at him from the corner of my eyes. He has a wide smile on his face and something that looks like awe. I pick my head up, turning to him in confusion before he tips his head across from us. When I look in that direction, I see Nick and Vince both passed out. Nick is cuddled up on Vince's shoulder with his hand resting on his chest. They're faces look so peaceful and I'm so damn happy they got together. Jenson and I knew long before either of them that there was something there. Although, neither of us thought Nick was going to be the one to initiate. They compliment each other perfectly.

I smile again before looking back at Jense to show him I agree with how cute they look. But when I turn my head towards him, I catch his stare aimed at my face. Before I can decipher the look in his eyes, he flinches, shakes his head, and then leans back into his seat as he looks out the window. *What the hell was that about? Do I have something on my face?*

As the plane hits the tarmac, I rub my face wondering if maybe I had some of the graphite on me but I could never locate it. *Oh well, I'll get it later.*

It takes all of ten minutes to land and exit the plane. We are definitely in a private airport or something similar. There's no one here except for us, and two black Escalades parked about 40 feet away. The driver steps out of one of the SUVs before opening up the back door and allowing another man to get out.

A man in a clean, pressed black suit steps out; his face an expressionless mask. I'd be lying if I said he didn't scare me a little. Or a lot. His whole aura screams power and danger. His jet black hair is shaved close on the sides and is longer up top, slicked back and shining in the afternoon sun.

We walk as a group but allow Vince to take the lead in greetings. He sticks out his hand, grasping the man's in a brief but firm handshake. "I'm Vince. Nice to meet you. Thanks for your help."

The other man's eyes widen in recognition and smiles while returning his shake. "Enzo. You look just like your old man. It's uncanny."

With a chuckle, they break apart and Vince turns to each of us, making official introductions. "Enzo, this is Nick, Cory, and Jenson." He nods to each of us in turn and we shake hands.

Enzo claps his hands together before stepping aside, and waves us into the SUV. "Please. We have much to discuss and I'm sure you know, time is of the essence."

We pile in the back two rows and head out of the airstrip. Enzo talks, all business, the entire ride. Within thirty minutes, we're turning down a dirt road with huge trees on each side. We've been driving through a heavily wooded area for the last half of the trip but now, we're right in the middle of it.

Just up ahead, I see a huge gray stone wall spanning the left and right side of the dirt road; disappearing into the trees. The walls have to be at least 12 feet high and have coils and coils of steel wire on top. Connected to the walls is a thick steel gate. It's one long, plain piece so you can't see through to the other side. A guard post sits on the right of the drive but I also spot four other armed guards hiding in the woods.

The guard in the post peers into the car as the driver rolls down the back window, allowing Enzo to nod at him. He turns around and presses some buttons before the gate begins to open with a whir. The space opens just enough for the SUV to pop through before immediately closing when the second SUV follows behind.

We drive another two minutes before the wooded area opens up to reveal a huge two-story farmhouse. The dirt road makes a large loop around a gorgeous cherry blossom tree with an intricately designed garden surrounding it.

The left side of the house shows fields further than I can see. The right side boasts of multiple, gargantuan greenhouses. We're talking a hundred feet in length, each. *Pretty sure we all know what grows in there.*

The car comes to a stop in front of the most beautiful mansion I have ever seen. Not that I've seen a lot but, wow. This house is ridiculous! Clean light stone covers the entire exterior with the exception of the black roof and ornately designed glass front door. *Oh, excuse me, double door.* The glass is slightly tinted with the few swirls of black running over them that give it just enough pop.

The house is at least two-stories and probably three times as wide as ours. Not that ours is anything to scoff at. We have plenty but this is...extreme. The middle section of the house boasts a balcony, guard included, that appears to lead into a bedroom or something. The sides of the house also have their own balconies that, judging by the time it takes for each guard to appear and reappear, wrap at least halfway around the house on each side.

The driver opens our door and we follow Enzo out of the car. I didn't even see that a man was standing by the front door, as well. There is far too much to look at and it's kind of hard to concentrate.

When we reach the man, his face breaks out into a smile and Enzo pulls him into a hug before giving him a gentle peck on the cheek. He then turns to us, waving his hand out before saying, "Bello, this is Sal's little boy. Well, Wes, now. Anyway, this is Vince and these are his friends, Nick, Cory, and Jenson." He pauses and returns his gaze back to the man before saying, "And this is Rocco." His smile beaming at

Rocco tells us all we need and it's crazy to see some gang leader living in a mansion being so open around strangers. But, good for him. Fuck what anyone else thinks.

Once handshakes are complete, Enzo nods towards the door and we follow in behind him and Rocco. We enter the foyer and the guys and I immediately freeze. *Jaw, meet floor.* Not only is this place even more massive on the inside, but it's pristine. Like, I feel like I need a shower before coming in even though I took one before boarding the plane.

The flooring consists of white marbled squares lined with two inch thick black marble. On each side of the foyer is a staircase that curves up to the second floor landing. The stairs themselves are bright white and are enhanced by the black swirls intricately designed in the railing. The landing then leads to a mini-bridge; to the back of the house, I presume.

Enzo leads us straight ahead, under the second floor landing, and into a huge "sitting room", *so posh*. The walls and lighting are decorated in whites and creams. The furniture consists of four, white high-back chairs, a navy couch, and a navy chaise lounge. The couch sits in front of the floor-to-ceiling windows boasting tall navy curtains; currently opened wide allowing for the sunshine to bathe the room in natural light. The room is covered in a navy and cream swirled carpet with a few small end tables placed next to each sitting area.

Just outside the windows, I catch a glimpse of the impressive pool area and what appears to be gardens. Before I have more time to get lost in the opulence of the place, Enzo and Rocco take a seat in two of the high-back chairs next to each other. Vince and Nick sit on the opposite side of the room, facing them, in the other two high-back chairs while Jenson and I take a seat on each end of the couch.

Enzo leans back and appraises us silently before looking at Rocco. After a moment, Rocco dips his head and Enzo turns his head back towards us. "How much do you know about our little operation?"

His brow lifts in question as his head tilts, no doubt assessing our honesty.

"We know enough. Dad didn't want to divulge too much because he knows this life is dangerous but we need the help. He also only knows what happened years ago so I'm assuming things have probably changed. With all due respect, I don't give a damn about what you all do, above board or otherwise. My only concern is getting Annie back." Vince's words never waver; authority and conviction obvious in his speech.

Rocco grins and glances quickly at Enzo who has yet to move a muscle. Not so much as a tick of his jaw. Suddenly, his laughter booms around the room and echoes off the high ceilings. Rocco chuckles and shakes his head but I still can't figure out if it's a good laugh or a dead laugh.

Enzo regains his composure before straightening himself. "You are so much like Sal it's hilarious. He, too, ran to bigger and badder for help because of love." My brows raise in surprise and I look over at Vince who looks equally surprised.

"What do you mean?" Enzo doesn't even answer, instead shaking his head with a fond smile. "No matter, son. But tell me, is she worth it? I know what you all do. I had my people check each of you out. Sal may have basically taken you under his wing when you were all teens but you all still turned out straight-laced, honorable men."

He levels a look at Vince before adding, "And *you* are an officer of the law. A good one, at that. So, before we move on, I need this one answer: Is she. Worth it. All? Lives, careers, futures?"

He lets the question settle in the air but none of us so much as flinch. In fact, we don't even look at each other. Instead I answer for us, "She's worth more than this lifetime or the next. We know we're moving into gray territory, we just don't care. We're getting her out of there come hell or high water. It may take us longer without your help, but we will still get it done because *she* means *everything*."

I see the others nod in my periphery, already knowing we were on the same page the moment we started planning this suicide mission. The simple fact is, life isn't worth living without her, and we will go to the ends of the Earth to find her.

Enzo and Rocco grin wide, nodding their heads, and begin to stand. Enzo turns towards Rocco, whispering something in his ear, before turning back to us. "Hope you're ready, because now that we have someone on our side who knows the ins and outs of the area, Lukas' little street gang will be wiped off the map within the week." His smirk curls mischievously as his eyes reveal wrath combining with determination.

"Now, if you'll follow me, we'll meet part of my team and start planning. We have a few hours before dinner is ready so if you need a snack or beverage, please let me know. My wife would kick my ass to Timbuktu if I didn't play the perfect host in our home." He mumbles the last part sarcastically, but the creepy grin from before vanishes as a genuine, loving smile appears.

We move to follow him out of the sitting room, into the right wing of the house. But I couldn't wrap my head around what he said. *He has a wife? But we saw him kiss Rocco, right? Maybe an arranged marriage or a convenience thing.* I shrug it off, shaking my wayward thoughts away as we continue to pass doors, upon doors, upon doors.

We finally stop at the last door in the hallway. Unlike the others, which were stark white, this one is all black and has a pin pad as well as a fingerprint scanner. The locks clack open as Enzo's identity is confirmed, and the door opens wide to a tech room. Monitors, tracking devices, things I can't even name fill the space along with three other men and one female. They are all sitting at a black conference table doing, whatever, on their own tablets.

Enzo quickly makes introductions before announcing that they will be helping us. He looks at each person in the room as he states that all information, known and found, is to be shared and planning needs to be agreed upon before continuing. He is so unlike any type of boss or leader I have ever known. His team is clearly a cohesive unit; one where everyone has ideas and everyone participates based on their strengths. *I guess I understand how he earned his loyalty.*

We all sit around the room, opening our own devices and immediately jump into what we know, what they know, and what our next steps should be. We split up the tasks needed to find where Lukas may be running his operations from; or even where he's sending his products to. Hope and excitement bubble up because we are *finally* moving forward, and we're closer than ever to getting our girl back.

19

Annie

For the love of all things holy, why does everything hurt? I groan as I slowly rouse from the shittiest nightmare ever. I bring my hands to my head and massage my temples but wince on contact. *Oh no.*

My eyes snap open and realization crashes around me. My nightmares are very real; and very painful.

I'm apparently back in my solo cage. I move to face the door but a sharp pain startles me, causing me to look down at my belly. My light blue Chemise has now been torn in half; just below my mom boobs. My flabby stomach has dried blood smeared down it but I can't tell where the marks end and the messes begin.

I cautiously make my way to stand, letting the wall support me. I have to lean against it for a moment as the room spins and bile creeps up my throat.

Once I breathe through the nausea, I peer down at my belly. There's nothing else in here so I whip the leftover pieces of my top off my head and lightly dab away at the blood until an undeniable pattern is revealed. *Ok, not pattern, word.* Even upside down I can clearly see that fuckhead carved the word "cunt" into my stomach. It's not super big but it's big enough to read. If I had to guess I would say it's about an inch tall and maybe four inches wide.

Tears begin filling my eyes and I can't help but wonder what the guys would think. I scoff at my own absurdity. I'm trapped, in a cell, forced to help these bastards train girls to be trafficked and I'm sitting here worried about what the guys will think of all the *pretty* new scars I have? *Jesus. Maybe I* am *having some kind of mental breakdown.*

I spend the next, however long, thinking about my mom, my kids, my students, my guys. I think about the time in middle school when my mom took me to the Renaissance Festival and we ate way too much food, walked around to all of the little shops, and watched as many shows as we could fit in. She even bought me a handmade scarf from a woman who was using an honest-to-God spinning wheel to make it. It was absolutely mesmerizing. In fact, I still have the scarf in my closet. A smile curls on my face as I slowly slide down the wall until I'm sitting on the ground, remembering just how amazing that day was to me.

The memory transforms into the day my girls were born. Finding out I was pregnant was a surprise but when the ultrasound tech said "*babies*", my soul briefly left my body. I was so scared and starting to panic, but she just waved that little wand around to get their first pics. One was a little jelly bean, looking relaxed, but the other looked like she was waving. My heart stuttered and I knew right then, they were mine and I was theirs; no matter what.

I let the tears running down my face go. I don't even bother trying to wipe them away as I allow myself this moment of catharsis, of joy, of peace.

I then sink into the memory of Josh being born; him coming out blue and not breathing before being rushed to the NICU. I didn't even get a chance to hold him and my heart shattered, right there on the operating table. I remember waking up some time later and panicking, crying for the nurse to let me see my baby. She had to rush over and calm me down, giving me more meds as I had lost too much blood during my c-section. She told me I needed to rest but reassured me he was doing well. The next day, they *finally* let me try to get up for their little standing test. I definitely pushed myself too hard but, I didn't care. Once I was approved, I had a nurse wheel my down there and I finally got to hold him. In fact, I held him until they physically forced me to go back to my room to rest.

Ironically, I don't think I've had a day of rest since. Those little turkeys have me absolutely wrapped around their fingers; and they know it.

My eyes begin to get heavy as my body fights exhaustion. I slide the rest of my body down to lie on the floor, not giving a shit that I'm now naked, and let the cool concrete ground me.

The last memories that flit through my mind are from the night I first met the guys. After my embarrassing run-ins with Cory and Jenson, I never would have imagined how amazing that night would end up. I remember their hands on my body, grinding to the music. Their lips on my skin, lighting me up inside. But, mostly, I remember how I felt completely and utterly seen, safe, and theirs. I hope I get to see them again. Even if I'm too damaged, too broken, to be theirs. I just want to see their smiling faces and smoldering eyes one more time.

I wake up gasping and sputtering for breath. The shock of the freezing water jolts my body and causes pain to explode from the various cuts that threaten to re-open. Self-preservation takes over and I feel myself backing into the corner and curling my knees against my chest. I shiver violently for a few breaths before I finally manage to look up and see who's to thank for the worst wake up call ever.

Lukas is standing there, seething, with a now empty bucket that continues dripping on the floor beneath him. His eyes are wild and dark like the night I left him; the one that I frequently visit in my nightmares.

The longer I stare, eyes wide and whole body trembling, the more *real* terror slithers through my body. I can immediately tell the human Lukas isn't here. No, this is the demon one. The one who can't be swayed, can't be coddled, and definitely can't be reasoned with.

We stay like that, neither of us moving and nothing but our heavy breathing filling the space, for at least five minutes; maybe longer.

His chest continues heaving and his nostrils are flaring like some kind of deranged bull. *Maybe he'll shapeshift.*

I have to bite the inside of my cheek to not laugh at my ridiculousness. I have clearly read way too many fantasy novels. *Focus, Annie! Now is not the time to be poking the* bear.

And. I. Lose it. The absolute absurdity of my mind never ceases to amaze me. Being off my meds has really done a number on my noggin. I don't remember being this flighty before. Well, maybe I was. Either way, it's just *really* not helpful right now.

My laughter rings out in my little dungeon in hell, causing me to unravel my body until I'm facing the ground, trying to catch my breath. Each time I look at him, his face gets a deeper shade of red, his body physically vibrates in anger and his facial expression clearly shows he's not only confused, but is steadily climbing from angry to enraged. *Looking like a pissed off little bull; or bear.*

I try so hard to hold it in but, I just can't. I try erasing the images my mind conjures up of how much uglier he would get if he shapeshifted. Logically, I know I need to chill so I try to breathe through the breakdown I'm obviously having. Once I think I'm calmer, I peer back at him, hoping it will snap some sense of self-preservation into me.

No dice; I just start laughing again.

With a roar that definitely couldn't be human, he launches the bucket at the wall over my head. It pings off my shoulder and the contact sends pain through my whole arm, effectively snapping me out of my laughing fit.

He towers over me in three long strides and I have to lean my head all the way back just to maintain eye contact. "What the fuck is so funny?" His spit lands on my face and it's all I can do to physically restrain myself from wiping it off. I just continue to stare at him, moving as little as possible, while trying to regain my breathing.

When I don't give him any kind of answer, he reaches down, grabs a hold of my hair and lifts me to stand. I yelp in pain as I feel some of the hair rip straight from my scalp. My legs wobble under me but I try my best to control it.

His eyes are still swallowed in darkness as his temper boils over. He scans his eyes down my body in disgust before quickly turning away; his hand still attached to my hair. I have no choice but to let him lead me by my hair, causing me to face down and bend slightly at the hips. The floor beneath me turns from my, now wet, cell to the hallway and I see the stairs come into view.

Although I stumble a few times due to the awkward position, I manage to make it to the main training room with most of my hair still attached to my head.

He marches me towards one of the cells where a young woman named Yelena lies in a fetal position in the corner. He opens the door, and shoves me in, causing me to trip and fall on my knees. By the time I whip my head back towards him, he's slamming the door shut and locking it in place. He walks away for a moment before returning with another blue chemise and a first aid kit, throwing them both at me before spitting, "Do your job, bitch." He turns on his heel and stalks away.

I hold my breath, listening to his retreating footsteps before the main door opens with a creak, and bangs closed. I hurriedly throw on the stupid chemise, ignoring the way my whole body protests, and rush over to Yelena. I lean down to make eye contact so she knows I need to check her out and get her fixed up. I've been with this group long enough that they know I won't start cleaning or touching anything on their body, including their hair, until they give me consent. Even if it's just a slight nod. They've been through enough.

After a moment, she seems to come back to herself and reveals a small relieved smile. She hands me her arm to check over and I get to work cleaning the cuts, scrapes, and rubbing ointment on the bruises.

As I finish packing up the remaining supplies, her eyes fill with tears and she looks straight into my eyes before whispering, "Can I have a hug?"

I don't know why but it throws me for a loop. Most people never want to be touched again after the shit they've been through. Hell, it took my mom two years to be able to hug me without me flinching. But, if I've learned nothing else in this hell, it's that we all process trauma differently.

Some of us disassociate, some ramble on about nothing important just to fill the silence, some cry, some rage, but at the end of the day, we're all doing what *we* need to survive. Our trauma isn't the same, and even if it is, we aren't. So how we cope with trauma looks different, too.

I realize I let too much time pass without giving her an answer and she looks so hurt and dejected. I put on my most gentle smile before whispering, "Of course."

Her eyes flash up to mine in surprise before I nod to the spot on the wall next to her. She nods her head quickly and I move my back against the wall, sitting with her side-by-side. Then I put one arm behind her neck and the other in front, just at the top of her chest so it's not crushing her airway. I bring both hands together on her left shoulder and gently hold her. She leans her head down on my chest as we both begin to softly cry.

And we stayed there, on the disgusting floor, in this deplorable dungeon, until exhaustion carries us away.

20

Vince

It's 10:00 am and I've already had three cups of coffee. We've spent two days planning with Enzo and his people. Two days talking strategy, viewing every type of map of Clear Lake and surrounding areas known to man, and conferring with the guys he already had in place trying to infiltrate the Black Thorns.

So far, one has made it as a low-level lackey, not getting much information other than orders as a drug runner but he's been making friends so, we'll see. The other guy caught one of the leader's attention after he put a bullet in some guy's head for trying to break into one of their warehouses. The good news is, he's supposed to be meeting with someone tonight and can hopefully get us a location soon.

Enzo ordered a group of his men to go and scout around since they know and understand all things criminal underworld. I realize I should absolutely be uncomfortable by the casual conversations I'm having with a huge player in the underworld, but I can't be bothered to. I just want to find Annie.

As it turns out, Enzo has turned Dad's gang into a very successful and powerful syndicate up here in Illinois. He moved his main headquarters to Sawyerville as he took more gangs under his wings. He has people spread out all over Illinois and spanning into Missouri, Indiana, Tennessee and Kentucky. I was also mildly surprised to hear he made friends with Cosa Nostra and a few other major crime groups.

Our first night here, we were introduced to Enzo's family. It was so unnerving to see the Don of a huge crime syndicate relaxed and, apparently, very in love. We already knew about Rocco but we also met his wife, Gina, and their other partner, Matteo. The way she blushed at all of their attention made my heart ache for Annie. I wanted to shower her like that; make her feel loved every day we have left on this Earth.

Gina was hilarious and so damn sweet. All of these hardened bastards turned to putty the moment she entered a room. Right after grace, she immediately addressed our confusion about the relationship situation; although I thought we had hidden it well. For the first twenty minutes of dinner she told us the story about how they saved her and a bunch of girls from a trafficking ring. She didn't have a family so they let her stay until she could get on her feet, gave her a job, all of it.

Then, she slowly fell for each of them. The more they softened towards her, the harder she fell. After winning the war against the bastards that took her, they decided they wanted forever. So, they gathered their closest friends and had a commitment ceremony. On paper, she's married to Enzo, but she's equally committed to each man.

Their story filled me with so much hope. I don't think any of us really thought about marriage being an option but, after spending time with Enzo and his family, maybe it is. The guys and I have been into sharing women for about six years now. It started on a drunken night, then again when we were sober the next day. And, I don't know, we just preferred it that way.

Watching a woman fall apart over and over again by our hands, to have her submit complete control over her body, her heart, her pleasure... Mmm. Nothing else can compare.

Over the years, we've had a few relationships, one-on-one and group, but Amber was our last long-term situation. She had moved in and we all showered her with every bit of love and affection we had. But, in the end, it wasn't enough.

Now, with Annie, I can feel the difference between them. I cared for Amber, but I'm *consumed* by Annie. Just thinking of her not being with us makes me want to rip my own heart out. I can't stand her not being here but, more than anything, I abhor that she's *there*.

A phone ringing brings me out of the abyss and I hear Enzo answer. I can only hear his side of the conversation and it's all boss-level phrases. "Yes....Ok...Are you sure?...Send it."

He hangs up and immediately turns toward the rest of us sitting around the tech room. "Alright, just heard from one of my guys. They're moving a shipment out *tonight*. Apparently a couple of their guys are down so they had to bring in some help. Lukas specifically asked for Mikas after hearing that he took that guy out for snooping around the warehouse."

His phone pings and he checks it before walking over to the laptop that is mirrored on the large screen on the wall. He clicks on the map of the Clear Lake area and types in the address that was sent to his phone. The pin drops on a residential lot that backs up to Nassau Bay.

"Shit." I spin around to see Nick pulling at his hair. "That's why they couldn't get a lead on where he's shipping out of."

I know my face shows the confusion I'm feeling but he just shakes his head and steps to Enzo. "May I?" Enzo waves him to the laptop and Nick immediately starts clicking buttons. Satellite images begin to zoom in on the location and I *finally* see it.

The house sits on the end corner of a cul-de-sac that backs up to the bay. It has a huge boat docking space directly on the bay. Additionally, each house on the street has a dock in the back, giving this house not just one docking area, but two. To make matters worse, directly across from the side of the house that backs up to the bay, is the Nassau Bay Peninsula Wildlife Park. A park that has almost no foot traffic past dusk. It makes it all too easy to move things under the cover of night. *This explains so damn much.* "They must be taking the shipments to a secondary location to offload."

Enzo snaps his eyes to mine but he's not seeing me. He's seeing past me; thinking. After a moment in complete silence, Matteo snaps his fingers before walking over to Nick. "Can you pull up shipping manifests?"

Nick glances at me in question and I nod my head. We're so far from lawful activities right now that there's no reason to stop at accessing shipping manifests illegally.

Nick turns around and immediately starts clackin' away. Within twenty seconds, the screen fills with a ridiculous amount of information. Matteo walks over to the screen and begins telling Nick what to filter. "Ok, filter out anything that isn't set to be in the Gulf tonight or tomorrow morning."

The number of options drops dramatically which has my heart beating faster. "Ok, now filter out anything that is a fishing boat, yacht, cruise line, or tanker." The number plummets even further.

We stand there reading the list before Nick moves the cursor back to filter and takes out Ultra Large Container Vessels. When Enzo asks why, Nick explains that they are the largest and there's no way a shitty gang leader, no matter how evil, would have the ability to turn a UCLV captain or crew. Only true Mafia members have that kind of pull. We all nod in agreement as the numbers drop again.

Rocco stands abruptly and asks, "Can you locate ship GPS logs?" Nick turns his way and cocks his head. "Like, cross-filter this list with ones that have stalled out in or near Galveston for longer than necessary to possibly load or unload cargo?"

Rocco nods eagerly like it's the best idea ever. My brows raise at the insane suggestion but also at the fact Nick was able to decode Rocco's odd question. I wouldn't in a million years have thought this bastard was that cunning but as the filters on the screen run, and the numbers dwindle further, I realize just how far out of our PDs wheelhouse this really was. Apparently Lukas is a lot fucking smarter than I gave him credit.

Within a few seconds, the screen now shows three possible options. My heart is beating so loudly that I can barely hear anything in the room. Nick and Rocco are saying something to each other but I only hear parts of it. Something about similar crews over the last year. During my next blink, one ship disappears from the screen.

The tension and excitement are thrumming through the air. *Two ships! Two fucking ships that Lukas may be using.* I stare at the information on the screen. Reading and re-reading until my eyes begin to blur.

Then, I see it. "That one!"

I guess it came out more forcefully than I wanted it to since I noticed the guys around me jump. I don't bother with an apology as I dash over to the screen and tap on the second ship on the list. Nick quickly clicks on it and brings up a list of the ports it's docked at over the last two years. He also has the system highlight similarities; right down to Captain and crew names. But the information I focus on is the frequency in which they make late night stops, near Galveston, for long periods of time.

"That's it. I agree." Enzo states. "Between the timing is the middle of the night and how often it stalls on those exact coordinates, about once every three-four weeks. Yeah, that's not a coincidence."

Cory stands with his hand rubbing his cheek, eyes narrowed and head tilted; his typical 'thinking face'. "Ok. Ok. So, during the periods that it stops, where is it traveling to and from?" Nick click-clacks away before a pin lands on Port Liberty Bayonne, New Jersey.

Matteo barks out a laugh while Enzo and Rocco chuckle and shake their heads. "What? Why is that funny?" I really have no idea. This is so far over my head that I am absolutely feeling like a useless sack of... "Buongiorno amico."

I whip my head around to see Enzo is talking on the phone. He walks around the room, confidence oozing from him with every step. His shoulders are pulled back, his left hand rests in his pocket casually, and his face holds a slight smirk.

He continues rattling off something in Italian. I have no clue what the hell he's saying but his smirk widens into a smile as he speaks. He walks over to the screen and rattles off the name of the ship and I hear him say "port" but I don't catch anything else.

He stays quiet for a moment, nodding his head as the other person talks. Enzo's smirk tilts into a devilish grin and he says, "Lukas O'Brian." Again, he's quiet while the other person speaks before suddenly saying, "Ci sentiamo presto." He moves the phone from his ear, clicks the button, and flashes a predatory grin that probably makes most people shit themselves.

"Well boys, looks like our friends in the Cosa Nostra weren't aware that our little friend has been using their ports to run his trafficking shipments." He claps his hands, the sound echoing around the room, and begins rubbing his hands together like he's an eager child about to dive into some cake.

"Holy shit." Is all I can respond to. Not only is this bigger than all of the HPD, this is FBI level bigger. "Ok, so what do we do, now?"

Enzo looks at each of us before stepping up to the table and sliding into a chair. "Now, we get ready. They're going to take care of their area and we'll do our part here. The ship is already on its way. We need to get to Clear Lake and fast. I'm thinking the house is the best bet."

His phone beeps with a message and he pulls it from his pocket, swipes the screen and grins like a damn maniac. "Oh my luck. We have two places. My *friend* wanted to thank us for the tip. He sent us the address to a warehouse they tracked back to some of the guys in Lukas' little gang."

My knees give out and I stumble my way over to a chair. *I can't believe we're really this close. This damn close.* I look up at Cory, Jense, and Nick and see the emotions racing through their minds. We all take a few deep breaths and let the feeling sof relief mixed with excitement wash over us.

Jense, Cory, Matteo, and Rocco come to sit at the table and Nick stays by the laptop. I nod at each of them before looking at Enzo. "Alright. What's the plan?"

21

Cory

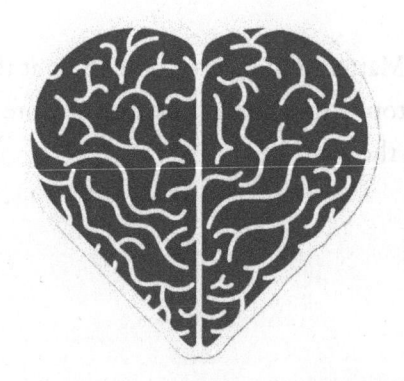

Three hours ago, we departed Enzo's plane; dusk painted the sky in pinks and oranges as the deeper shades of night crept in. We spent the trip reviewing our plan with Enzo, Rocco, Mateo, and Gina; who fought tooth and nail to be part of this. Enzo ultimately caved when she told him that none of us will ever come close to understanding what Annie may have seen or been through. But she does, she knows, and she may be the best person to help.

The thought of Annie not even wanting our help just about shredded my heart. But, if there's even a tiny possibility she'll want Gina's help, then that's what she'll get. I can only hope and pray that our imaginations are wildly inaccurate. *Maybe he's just had her locked in a comfy room like Rapunzel?* I scoffed at myself. I knew better. I just didn't want to think too hard about it. I couldn't do that and stay focused.

As soon as we landed, a herd of SUVs waited for us. Enzo's people climbed in the second one while we were ushered into the third. There were seven in all. A couple of minutes after we left the airstrip, Jense broke the silence. "Holy shit. This is really happening. Like, right now."

I could tell he was a bundle of nerves and energy. His leg was bouncing a million miles a minute and he kept looking out the window like he was taking in every detail of the scenery. We live here so it's not like there's anything new to see.

Not even thinking about it, I laid my hand on his bouncing knee and squeezed gently. His knee immediately stopped bouncing and he whipped his head down to look at my hand. I considered taking it off but something inside told me not to.

After a tense moment, his eyes traveled to mine and he gave me a thankful grin before turning back out to look at the window. I blew out a breath, relieved he didn't react negatively.

As soon as I did, I forgot how to breathe all together. I looked down to try and process what I was feeling. *Holy shit, he laid his hand on mine!* I watched, entranced, as his fingers ever so slowly slid between mine before he squeezed. We rode the rest of the way, not bringing attention to it, but also not letting go.

Twenty minutes later, we pulled into a hotel just off Nasa Road 1. Ours and two other SUVs parked, spread across the lot, while the other four kept going. The plan was for them to trade out the SUVs with more inconspicuous vehicles that were scattered around the area. They would then wait to meet us later at different rendezvous points.

Most of us wore regular clothing, some wore suits, and some looked like they're beach-bound. The goal was to not attract attention. We would all spend the next hour slowly checking in, then meet in Enzo's room to finalize the plan.

The guys and I barely spoke while we waited, all of us too engrossed with thinking about our roles in the plan. There were six different vans scattered around the parking lot for us. Three would go to the warehouse; 4 minutes away. The other three were headed to the house; 9 minutes away.

The guys and I were split between the two groups. Each group would leave with three different vans; one unmarked, one for an electric company, and one for a water company. The plan was to have two of the three vans empty, except for drivers. One van would take victims we may find to the hospital. The other would be for those who may need medical attention. Enzo already had doctors waiting in another discrete warehouse; almost 10 minutes away from both locations.

Additionally, Enzo already had two groups of ten men waiting at median locations to follow the convoy once we gave the signal. In total, each group had over 20 men ready to flatten this asshole and everything he had.

We also agreed that no prisoners were needed from this little escapade. The thought of going in there to actually kill and destroy should have made me highly uncomfortable. I know this. My brain says so. But, I just don't care. They took our girl; and Lord knows how many others.

Vince reminded us that taking a life is far different than just thinking about it. The ramifications that can come from that, psychologically, are a heavy burden to bear. I get that. I understand wholeheartedly. But, to get Annie, it doesn't matter. I'd deal with internal fallout later if it meant having her back in my arms.

The closer we got to leaving, the more my stomach churned. *What will we find? What if she's not there?*

Vince cleared his throat before we went to our final meeting in Enzo's room. "Listen guys. I, this is..." He exhaled heavily as he rubbed his hands up and down his face. "This is going to be hard. We all know how to fight, we all know how to shoot, but *training* and *doing* are two different things. Yes, this is about Annie, but it's also about so much more than that. There's always a possibility we get caught. *And*, even if we are taking out a group of vile bastards, that doesn't make what we're doing legal. This is *major* jail time."

He took in a deep breath, glancing at each of us before he continued. "If you want to stay behind, please, *please* do. Do not go into this thinking you *have* to. You are more than welcome to wait here, where it's safe, and you can have some sort of plausible deniability. I would one thousand percent support you and absolutely no one would say anything if you didn't go through with this part."

He pauses for a moment before turning to Nick and smiling gently, "Nick, this means you, too. You don't *have* to be in the van to tap into security, someone else can do that while you talk them through it on the phone. I just, I just want everyone to really think about what's about to happen. It's no longer a conversation, it's an action. And it can't be undone."

We stood in silence for over a minute before Jenson shook his head and grinned. "I'm not going anywhere. We do this, like we do everything else; together. Am I scared? You bet your chiseled ass I am! But, I'm all in. For us *and* for Annie."

I found myself nodding along, straightening my back as I contemplated my words. The pieces of our plan flew around my head like jigsaw pieces and I could see each step clearly mapped up in my mind. "Yup. I'm in. Besides, Jense may be the better fighter, but I'm the better shooter." I winked cockily at Jense as I grinned smugly.

The tension lightened in the room for a brief moment as we chuckled. Once it died down, I nodded again, being serious this time and said, "I mean it. I'm all in. Period."

Nick was picking at the label on his water bottle, showing his only tell that he was nervous. He looked at each of us before tapping Vince on the shoulder, "I'm in. I need to be there. I want to be there. I'm not backing out. I'm going to have eyes on all of you and, hopefully, our girl. Let's do this."

With a final nod, Vince kissed Nick quickly, then brought Jense and I in for a bro hug. "All right boys, let's go get our girl."

And with that, we made our way to Enzo's room for last-minute plan reminders and to suit up. Even Nick will have a bulletproof vest and a gun; just in case.

22

Annie

A few hours ago, I was ripped out of the cell that I share with Jodie. My anxiety ramped up as I saw all of the women being lined up, shackles adorning their ankles and wrists. They were lined up by their chemise color; red in the front, followed by black, then white.

The bastard who took me from the cell held onto my arm so tightly it left bruises. After flinging me towards the girls, he informed me that my job was to keep them in line and quiet. If they caused any trouble, they would be punished and so would I.

We were ushered out of the dingy dungeon into another part of the creepy, old building. The only light we had was from the flashlight of the jackass leading us. Once we reached a wide metal door, he banged on it twice before he slammed something on the side. The door began rolling upwards, screeching as it went. It made my ears tingle with an irritation that skittered through my body.

The door opened to reveal a dark, empty metal box. Once we all crowded in, Jackass followed us, grabbing onto a thick, looped rope secured to the roof, then double tapped the metal wall next to us. The door we walked through began closing but the box we were in suddenly jolted forward, then quickly stopped, causing us to stumble. Jackass let go of the rope, clearly secured there so he wouldn't fall, and hopped out of the box. Without a word, he turned around and closed the door, trapping us in. Shortly after, we heard the heavy squeal of a latch, and click of a lock; signaling that we had no way out. Then, we were off.

I quickly surmised that we were being transported in some kind of box truck. It wasn't quite as big as an 18-wheeler but, still room enough for us to all sit down. Eventually, we lapsed into silence and just let our thoughts run wild. I couldn't see anything because it was so dark but I hummed out a tune. After a moment, a few of them started humming the tune with me.

At first, it caught me off guard because I hadn't even realized I was humming something specific. Once the song registered, I dropped the humming and started singing the actual lyrics, trying and failing not to laugh. Some of the other girls started giggling, others laughing out right, but many joined in as my stupid brain had apparently supplied the tune of Paint the Town Red by Doja Cat.

We continued singing during our trip. I let the other women choose the next couple of the songs. Some I knew, others I didn't, but it really didn't matter. For a brief moment in time, we were free; even if only in our minds.

Thankfully, we had ended our impromptu karaoke party by the

time we stopped moving. The last thing I wanted to do was get the women in trouble.

The door clicked and the screeching of a latch lifting pierced the air just before the door was flung open wide. A huge spotlight filled the space, blinding us. I squeezed my eyes shut as the heavy thumping of footsteps crowded the space. Startled gasps and screams rang out as the women were yanked up to stand.

My vision was just barely adjusting when Brute came pounding in like a damn gorilla. "Princess. Tell your bitches to shut up!" He roared. His voice echoed around the metal box.

I scrambled to my feet and marched over to him, tiny needles stabbing my legs and butt as they came back to life. "Listen here, Dickhead. First of all, maybe if you hadn't blinded us after keeping us in the dark it wouldn't have startled everyone. They would have reacted the way your stupid asses "trained" them." I sneered as I made air quotes and made sure he felt every ounce of hatred I had for him. "Secondly, *they* aren't bitches. The only bitches I see around here are *you* and your shitty thugs pretending to be men." I spit out the last few words hoping to have made my entire damn point.

The backhand I received made my cheek swell and my lip split, again. I slowly turned my head back towards him, smiling as wide as I could, while fluttering my eyelashes. "Aw Brutey, did I hurt your widdle feelings?"

While I held his fuming glare, I quickly darted a glance to the women. They were all quiet, standing perfectly still in a line outside of the metal box, warily watching the show. *Good. That's what I was hoping for.* I didn't have to order them around. I just needed to give them time to calm down while also taking the attention off of them. I was going to get the punishment either way; might as well make it worth my time.

Ten minutes, and a few whaps to the ribs later, we were put on the same boat I woke up on when I first was taken. *At least this time I was conscious.* The girls were all hustled into rooms, based on their chemise color, before being injected in the neck with something. I knew better than to ask but noticed how they all stayed semi-conscious while their eyes began to glaze over and lose focus.

Unlike my last ride on the boat, I was not placed in a room. They've had me sitting on this big white couch in the living room for over an hour.

I tried to not focus on where we were. I wasn't all that fond of large bodies of water where you can't see what's under you. Nope, not my jam. On top of that, it is terrifyingly dark out and the only light came from the water reflecting the beams from the spotlight.

Instead, I spent that time deep in some of my favorite memories. It's funny what perspective does for your mind. I realize that there's been so much evil and so much darkness in my life but, I still had things to live for. I still had reasons to smile, laugh, and to look forward to. My kids were far from this, safe and loved. My mom gets to watch my babies grow up. The guys just started this new venture with the youth center and, who know, maybe Vince will take these assholes down. Even if I'm not around to see any of it, I will choose to smile and be thankful for the time I did have.

A walkie crackled from somewhere outside, snapping me out of my daydreams and memories. Within seconds, I start seeing a myriad of light beams from flashlights dancing through the windows. A couple of jackasses walked through the door, not paying me any mind. One had a skeezy combover that screamed pedophile and the other was in desperate need of a trim; or a wash; or both. I notice they each have a gun in the back of their waistbands and a walkie clipped to their front hip.

A few moments later, the girls in black chemises were escorted out the door. They each had cuffs around their hands, and cuffs connecting each girl to the one behind her. Combover held a leash that was attached to a collar on Jenn's neck. None of the girls looked at me except Yelena. But, she wasn't looking at me, she was looking through me. Her eyes were vacant; empty.

I jumped to my feet and yanked on Yelena's cuffs. "What the hell? Where are you taking them?"

Combover turned around, sneering at me. "Fuck off, Bitch! Sit your ass down like the good little whore you are."

"No! Tell me where they're going! They're my responsibility and I'm not letting them go anywhere with *you*."

He dropped the leash and stomped over to me but I refused to cower. He snarled right in my face, his breath smelling of day old ashtray and cinnamon gum. "Seems like the little whore hasn't learned her lesson," he gritted through his yellow-stained teeth.

I quickly surveyed the room. It was just us and the girls; for now. None of the girls moved other than to sway due to the drugs in their system, or the rocking of the boat.

Just then, an idea came to me. It was stupid but, whatever, I was already in hell.

I did my best to curl my shoulders forward and dropped my head a little. "I, I'm so-sorry, sir. I just g-got scared. Lukas said not to let anything happen to them. I ju-just didn't know." I threw in a lip wobble and a sniffle in for good measure.

"Whatever dumb bitch. They're leaving so you go sit your ass on that couch and get out of our way."

I was nodding my head before he even finished. "Y-yes sir." I act like I'm going to step away just as he turns back towards the girls. I don't think; I just move.

A yank the gun from his waistband, raise it up, and pull the trigger. The bang that vibrates through space bounces between my ears along with the startled cries of the girls. Chaos descends around me and everything seems to move in slow motion. *Holy fuck. I shot someone.*

There is blood everywhere. Brain matter litters the floor; red splatters the white couches. The living room looks like a grotesque Jackson Pollock. *Oh shit, oh shit, oh shit!*

Arms wrap around me, abruptly bringing me out of my shock. I look up just in time to see Yelena trailing behind the others; right out the front door.

"Nnnooooo!" I fight and claw, kick and elbow. Whoever has me in his arms only grunts when a few hits land, but he never releases any of the pressure from my body.

I can hear men yelling from the walkies outside as a loud metal door slams shut. The guy who's wrapped around my back lifts me up just as the room fills with four other guys. I kick back under me and am rewarded with a grunted gasp. His arms relax just enough that I throw my head back; a satisfying crunch sounding out.

I'm unceremoniously dropped on the floor but, before I could go anywhere, two guys step up. They both wrench my arms behind my back, causing me to scream out as pain splinters through my arms and shoulders. I'm bent over, face parallel with the floor, when something stings me in the neck.

My vision doubles and my brain becomes foggy. My ears are ringing but I can't move. Like, I can feel everything, every heartbeat, every splinter of pain shooting up my arms. But, I have no control of my movements. *What the...*

All of a sudden, I notice the floor is rising to meet me. My head explodes in pain on impact but I can't bring my hand up to rub it or check if I'm bleeding. *Why didn't my hands come out to catch me? Why can't I move?*

I hear a growl coming from my left but can't get my head to turn so I can look at the person. Someone starts shouting, "Let's go! We gotta get out of here. Ham, call Lukas. Tell him his little project fucked up our drop. We still have whites and reds. And, uh, go ahead and tell him Kane is dead. Make sure he knows his little *bitch* killed him."

With that, I'm being lifted into the air, my head hanging

backwards at an angle that makes it hard to breathe. The guy carrying me maneuvers his arm under my head just enough to straighten it out before plopping me on the bed.

My heartbeat is so fast, so loud, so painful that I can't keep my anxiety in check. Each time I try, I remember that I can't move and it heightens again. I thought I knew hell, but apparently; I was so, very wrong.

23

Jenson- One Hour Ago

As soon as we step into Enzo's room, Nick begins hacking into local cameras at, near, and surrounding our two target locations. He quickly narrows down which devices had recordings he could access, then flies through footage to find the two cameras that have the best angles of each location. Within ten minutes he had scrolled through the last five hours of each recording.

While he did that we were all meeting the guys on our teams and discussing strategy. The sun had already set and we knew we had to move-in tonight.

I overheard Vince ask someone, "What's wrong?" The concern in his voice has me turning towards him, then following his line of sight to Nick. Nick's face is ghost-white and he's no longer typing away.

"Nick. What'd you find?" Hearing his name, he slowly raises his head, his eyes following last; like he doesn't want to stop looking at whatever is on the screen.

He swallows hard, his Adam's apple bobbing before he speaks. "They left."

Vince marches over to Nick and squats next to him. "Nick, I need you to focus. What did you see?"

His eyes begin to fill with tears as he slowly turns the computer around and clicks 'play' on the screen. We watch with rapt attention as seven men load multiple crates into the back of a truck. Nick moves the video twenty minutes forward before pushing play again. We all die a little as another truck is loaded with women; dressed in barely there lingerie.

We know right away; the one in blue, that's our Annie. Nick inhales a stuttered breath before announcing, "Th-this was just a little more than two hours ago; an hour or so after sunset. I scanned the surrounding area and this whole section of town dies before sunset. It really is the perfect location for him to hide his dealings." The more he talked, the stronger his voice was, but he couldn't hide the pain glimmering in his eyes.

The security cameras are shitty but we can tell there are slashes in varying stages of healing along her arms and legs; her head hung down in defeat. I don't even need to look around to know how my brothers feel. I know they share the debilitating fear that we're seeing her for the last time.

Thankfully, being the boss he is, Enzo pulls us out of our emotions and reminds us of the bigger picture. There was no way to get here earlier to stop them without resources and a plan in place; especially since we just found most of the information this morning. If she *does* get transferred to the other ship, the Cosa Nostra is already waiting to intercept them. This is *our* area. *We* hit Lukas here, and we need to trust that they'll handle their end.

Vests are passed out along with weapons each person is comfortable with; guns, knives, fucking grenades. *Hell yeah! I've always wanted to throw one of these.*

Vince and Nick are heading over with Rocco and Matteos' teams to the house. Cory and I are going with Enzo and two more teams to the warehouse. Each group gathers around one of the two twin beds in the room to look at blueprints and maps their target location. We run through Plans A, B, and C, as well as codes the drivers will use over the walkies to communicate with each other.

Earpiece comms are then passed out so we can talk to others within our group. Nick will have an earpiece for each ear so he can communicate with both groups as needed. All the comms are connected together until we make it to our destination. Then, Nick will split the signals for the two groups. This way chatter or movement doesn't get confused between the groups. Once our comms are in place, we review entrances, exits, and evacuations.

Our last discussion focuses on wrap-up plans. Where to drop any innocents we encounter, where to take men who need medical attention, and where the rest of us will meet once we finish. My hands and fingers don't stop moving as go-time crawls closer. Energy thrums through my body. *I'm so fucking ready. This is it.*

The warehouse my group is going to seems to have been converted into one large space in the interior. But, to get to it, you have to pass through a corridor *and* another door. There also appears to be some other kind of open space but that's not detailed in the blueprint. We're very well aware that these blueprints probably don't detail much since this asshole is shady as shit.

With the exception of the loading docks, it seems like there's only one entrance into the primary space; which is where it gets tricky. We won't be able to see who's in there to prevent unnecessary casualties. We decide that smoke bombs are the best course of action to get in; after the initial door blast. We're basically going in blind after that.

As we do last minute equipment checks, my mind fills with thoughts of Annie. It hurts so much that she was taken away with the others. I really thought we were going to see her. I thought today was the day we would finally get her back. Knowing she's on her way with the others up North deflates me; just a little. I clear my head and remind myself that there are *very* powerful people waiting for their arrival. I'll see her soon.

Until then, I get to have a little fun destroying Lukas' shit.

Someone's hand on my shoulder brings me out of my daydream; starring me as Jason Statham in Wrath of Man. Vince is next to me and Cory stands across from me, looking like I feel. Some jacked-up mixture of disappointment and eagerness. *It really is a strange combination.*

Vince leans in and whispers, just loud enough for us to hear, "I know this sucks, but it's still the best course of action. We'll get her eventually, but we *need* to take down this asshole's operation while we can. We're in this together, right?"

He sticks his hand out and I grasp it without a second thought. Cory places his hand over ours and squeezes. "Together."

Five minutes later we're staggering our exit down the stairs, on either side of the building. With one last nod to Vince and Nick, Cory and I load up into our group's electric company van.

Nick's voice crackles over the comms, "Team 1: check." Then the rest of the teams check-in. "Team 4: check," I say when it's our turn. After all 6 teams give the green light, we pull out.

Enzo's voice filters through the comms, "Message from my guy. Something interrupted the transfer and they had to come back. Only some of the merchandise was moved."

A few seconds later, Nick comes through the line, "Confirmed. Group Alpha: I've confirmed five men going back. They unloaded eleven girls."

I confirmed, "Alpha team copy. Five-known targets."

Nick then responds, "Team Bravo: seventeen men total at the house. One took a girl in the house after everyone else unloaded. Too dark to see her but there's at least one innocent."

Rocco's voice confirmed before Nick rang out, again. "Team Bravo: 3 armed in the backyard, right against the house, 1 armed on the boat, 2 on each side of the house and 2 at the front door. Remaining 7, including Lukas, in the house."

Mateo confirms and comms go silent for the rest of the ride. We know Nick will tell us if something changes.

The van is charged with energy bouncing in, out, around, and through. I'm braced against the van's wall with Cory next to me. Hearing some of the women were brought back made me feel a tingle of excitement. Maybe one of them was her. *I could hope but, saving any of them would be fucking amazing.*

Within minutes, we're pulling up on the west side of the warehouse on Gemini. It's eerily dark but the few street lamps lighting the side street reveals a barely visible door to our right. When we circle the building we see a lone truck backed into the loading dock. It's the same one we watched leave a few hours ago in the video.

Enzo's voice comes online, "Team 4, set up. Teams 5 and 6, waiting for the signal."

I can hear my heart beating in my ears as my adrenaline comes to a crescendo. I can't hear my breathing, or the sounds of the van door sliding open. I can't hear our boots thumping on the ground as we make our way to the side of the building; just left of the door.

But I sure as hell hear the boom of the grenade I threw. *Show time!*

We sprint around the building into the gaping hole that used to be a door. I can feel Cory hot on my heels as another door appears in front of me. I stand to the side, count down on my fingers, then throw the door open, tossing in a smoke bomb before slamming it closed.

As the smoke curls under the door, and coughing ensues, Enzo barges through the door. He and another guy gracefully move through the smoke down the center of the room; sweeping their guns around the room as they move in sync.

Training my gun in front of me, I step left to clear this side. I spot someone clothed in all dark colors, barreling towards me. Knowing the girls are all barely dressed, I pop off a shot. The guy goes down with a partial grunt; then a thud.

Cory and another guy head off to the right. In seconds I hear more gunshots echo out, signaling how large this cavernous room is. I swiftly make my way down the entire left wall; well a row of cells. When I don't counter anyone else, I turn around and make my way back, rapidly scanning the cells and their inhabitants.

A couple more gunshots ring out as I hastily relieve the dead asshole of his keys and unlock the first cell. When I open the cell, a woman, maybe twenty-three, cowers in the corner. I hold up my hands, slowly lowering myself to the ground. "It's ok. I'm here to get you out. You're free, but we gotta go now. Do you know where everyone is? We can get them all but we need your help."

It takes her a moment but, as more of the smoke clears, her eyes widen and she gasps in surprise. I slightly turn my head and see that the man I killed is lying on the floor; blood pooling out of his head.

I slowly turn back to her, hoping she can see the sincerity in my eyes. "We know he was a bad man. We *want* to help. Please. We're actually trying to find someone..." I struggle to swallow around the lump of cotton that has apparently dried out my mouth.

"We love her. My friends and I. We traced her to these guys. Do you, do you know Annie?" Her eyes widen and she tilts her head. *God I hope she speaks English.*

After a tense moment in silence, I try again. "Annie? Blonde hair, bright blue eyes?"

She doesn't respond. I shake my head and exhale heavily. "Ok. It's ok but, we have to go. Ok?"

I slowly back out through the door, and lightly shake the keys in my hand towards the next cell. "I have to go unlock the other cells. I'll be back."

I turn to go to the next cell, nodding in her direction one more time. The gunshots have died down and I can hear the others coaxing women out of their cells. By the time I get to the third cage, the woman from the first cell tip-toes after me. I don't want to scare her off so I stay silent and open the next cage, then the last one that has two women in it.

I step back, looking between them all. I try to keep my voice gentle and calm but there is definitely a sense of urgency I need to convey. "We're here to help but we have to go. We have to leave *now*. We'll get you out safely but, we don't know if any more of *them* are coming back here. We need to leave, right now." I pointed towards the man I shot so they hopefully understand we aren't with those bastards.

The women slowly slide out of the cells, trembling and holding on to each other. I notice they're all wearing red or white. No one here has blue.

I briefly feel a stab of disappointment but quickly remember that these women are just as important. Their families probably miss them as much as we miss Annie. And, dammit, no one deserves this crap.

Tapping my ear piece I report, "Team 4; 6 left side. Comin' out." I look at all six women in front of me before nodding my head towards the door then gently wave them to follow me.

Right before I escort the women to the door, well hole in the wall, movement across the room catches my eye. I focus my attention across the room as Cory stumbles out of another door from the back up the room. He has a black eye and blood is dripping down his face from his lip and hairline, and blood splatters his body.

I want to run to him, make sure he's ok but the women are hesitating between me and the way out. Right before I make a run for it, I see another guy near him rushes to catch him; just as he passes out. The guy struggles for a second then whistles for one of the others to help. As bad as I want to go to him, I have to finish this part and Cory is in good hands.

I turn back to the women, give them a gentle smile, then lead them out of the building. The plain, black van and the water company van are both pulled up on the sidewalk, open and waiting. Enzo and some of his men are running around, grabbing blankets for the women to cover themselves, and coordinating which van will carry which passengers.

The women will all be transported to the hospital in the black van and their respective friends and family will, hopefully, be contacted quickly. Enzo already used his influence to ensure that no paperwork, or cameras, show who drops them off. We were drilled repeatedly not to give any names away and most of us are wearing thick beanies over our head with black smudging our faces to distort what they may see. That will keep police from finding out who saved them and, inevitably, who took out all of these assholes.

Any men who are wounded will be loaded up into the water company van and taken to a private office strip Enzo has set up. He has a team of doctors and nurses waiting to patch anyone up as quickly as possible. The rest of the men will head back to a meeting point on Nasa Rd 1; unless needed at the house.

Once all eleven girls are loaded up, water and snacks in hand, I turn to see Cory and two other guys climbing into the water van. I make the decision to go with Cory but, before I can take a step, something tugs at my sleeve.

The scared, brown-eyed girl I first talked to has crawled to the opening of the van, away from the group of women huddled on the far side. In a low voice she asks, "You know Annie?"

I turn towards her completely, my heart leaping in my throat. "Y-yes. She's my," I turn to point at Cory and meet her eyes again, "Our girlfriend. She has kids. I think she was wearing blue, right?"

The brown eyed girl nods vigorously, a tear leaking from her cheek. "You have to help her." Her pained whisper almost breaks me.

She turns to look at the other girls before facing me. Her eyes lock on mine, fear sketching lines across her forehead, "You have to help her. Sh-she helped us. But, she's in trouble. O-on the boat, she killed a guy. Th-They drugged us. She tried to stop the guy from taking the other group of women off the boat."

Her shoulders slump in defeat. But, then she shakes her head and continues. "I heard the gun go off and people were yelling. One of the other guys barged in and chained us to the cabinets in the room. He mumbled something about a crazy princess and he had blood all over his clothes and face. Then he said we had to go back. Wh-when we got back to the big house, he came back for us."

A shiver runs down her body as her eyes gloss over, lost in the memory. I reach in next to her and pull out one of the blankets, draping it over her shoulder. Her eyes flit back to me before she inhales deeply and continues. "The living room was so bloody. So, *so* bloody. But, we knew better than to ask."

She takes a shuddering breath, her eyes a little clearer than before and her voice just a little more steady, "S-sir. Lukas. He was there when we got off the boat. He was on the phone. I heard him say that one of the guys who attacked Camilla last week, well, he died today. Annie hurt him and his brother. She *did* something; she *helped*. Who's going to help *her?*"

Her eyes bounce erratically between mine as she fights to finish. "Lukas was madder than I've ever seen. He sounded possessed when he said it was time to end her training. I, I think he's going to kill her. They left her there. She never came back..."

Her voice had spiked with anxiety right before her words were broken on a sob. Tears cascade down her face as she throws her hands around; like her emotions just need some kind of outlet.

"Hey," I said gently, "Look at me." Her eyes swing open; lashes heavy from holding on to the tears.

I bend down just enough to be eye level with her, "Thank you. Thank you for telling me. Is it a big house with a big pool and a boat dock in the back?"

She nods her head adamantly and I give her the best smile I can. "Good, we have friends there *right now*. They'll get her."

She smiles just enough to show her appreciation before taking a steady breath. Then she crawls back to the corner of the van and huddles with the others. I move to walk back to the other van with Cory, but decide to turn back around. "Ma'am. What's your name?"

Her eyes widen briefly before her body relaxes. "Jodie".

I nod with a smile, "Thank you, Jodie. We'll get her but, for now, you worry about healing and being safe." I take a quick glance around to the others before adding, "All of you."

With that, one of Enzo's guys climbs into the driver seat while I close the door. I faintly hear him explain to the women where they're being taken as another guy climbs into the passenger seat. They roll out of the parking lot without a second glance.

I move back to the water van and climb in next to Cory. "I'm going with him." I look up at Enzo and he tips his head in understanding before shutting the door behind me.

The comm rings through my ear as we start our evacuation count; making sure we're all accounted for. Once the final man clears, we're leaving the shitty warehouse behind.

Not even half a block later, multiple booms filter through the windows and a huge fireball explodes into the sky. I swear I feel the ground rumble underneath the van.

With that feeling of finality, the van bounces its way right out of the warehouse area; inching closer to 145.

I lean down, pressing my forehead to Cory's sweaty head. His eyes are closed with dirt and blood caking his face. But, I can feel his semi-steady breaths and feel the beat of his heart through his chest. Closing my eyes, I inhale deeply, wrapping myself in the knowledge that he's ok; It's done. We made it out alive. We helped those women; saved them. *But, I killed a man. Cory's hurt and Lukas plans to kill Annie.*

I'm a jumbled mess of highs and lows. The anxiety, the fear, the rush of knowing we saved those women. It all collides in my heart and my mind like the perfect storm.

I stay there, unmoving, for the rest of the trip. Not a word is spoken by anyone during the entire ride. I hold on to my best friend, grunting in pain, and pray the others will make it out alive.

24

Annie

I'm not sure how long it's been since they threw me in here but I'm pretty sure whatever they gave me is starting to wear off. My anxiety over being unable to move has long since passed. It also helps that no one has been in here since dumping me on the bed.

At first, there was a lot of shouting and swearing and thumping from the big-footed ogres on board. But, it's been terrifyingly quiet ever since. Nothing more than the gentle thrum of the engine as the boat moves across the water.

It's left me far too long to consider just how far I've fallen. Even if by some miracle I get out of here and back home, what kind of mother am I? *I killed someone! Shot him without a second thought. I killed someone. He's dead. Like, actually dead.*

My vision blurs as tears make their way into my eyes. But, I don't deserve to cry. *I'm a monster; just like Lukas. I'm officially no better than any of these bastards. My kids are much better off without me.*

Numbness has become my friend, and not just the physical kind I've learned to hone. No, this is a murky, dark numbness that has filled my heart and taken over my soul. I don't even try to fight it. I just let it swallow me whole.

***

The door slams open, pulling me from my self-loathing, and rattling the cabinets around me. The guy from earlier, Ham I think, comes thumping down the stairs and into the room.

Whatever drug they pushed into me earlier is mostly worn off, but I'm so damn sluggish that I can't get my body to maneuver away from him fast enough. I shakily try to sit up and scoot away but my limbs can't hold my weight. My arms give up the moment I have them under me and I fall back, cracking my head on the cabinet behind me.

Before my vision fully clears, I'm being yanked by my feet to the end of the bed. I try to find purchase but there's something delaying the process from my brain to my arms. Ham barely catches me before my ass hits the floor, throwing me over his shoulder with a grunt.

I lay there suspended, upside down like a ragdoll, as my anxiety ramps up, again. I stare at my hands, willing them to move, to fight, to do fucking *something*. I release a low grunt as my right arm *finally* moves but it barely makes a tap on his back. I try again and again but continue to fail miserably.

Half-way through the living room area, I realize I can sort of lift my head. Sparks of hope ignite through me so I briefly give up on using my arms and try to use my legs, instead. I will my brain to send the right signals; trying with all my might to land a kick.

Then, we're plunged into darkness. The breeze from the water flips my chemise up and over my ass, causing goosebumps to skitter across my body. I didn't realize how cold it was earlier, but I can sure as hell feel it now.

I give up trying to kick Ham and raise my head as much as I can. I expected a marina or something but we've actually docked at a house. It's an enormous house with what appears to be a jaw-dropping outdoor kitchen, gazebo, and pool. I can't see much as the outside is only lit by the lights in the pool. But what I can see is absolutely stunning. Like one of those places that those YouTube guys would do an episode on.

I barely have time to take-in the rock feature/waterfall in the pool before we're entering the house. I drop my head when pain from the strain in my neck becomes too much. Now I'm forced to stare at the gorgeous white and gray marbled flooring.

I hate that I love it. It is *stunning*. But, the squeaking of wet shoes grates on my nerves, causing me to clench my jaw. I can hear shoes thumping and squeaking all over the room but can't figure out where they are, how many of them are here, or how big this place is.

The marble flooring makes way to dark wood, for just a few feet, before Ham suddenly steps up. A second later, I realize my body is bouncing more than it had been. Scanning my eyes around, I see that we're making our way up a set of stairs. Swirling wrought iron beams hold up the dark wood railing; matching the stupidly beautiful floors.

The bobbing of my head and body slows as wooden stairs make way to pristine light cream carpet. My brain unhelpfully provides an image of my kids running around on the ridiculously light carpet; completely destroying it in minutes. *Which is why I ripped all of mine out when we first moved in to our house. Ew.*

A door opens behind me and I'm hastily thrown onto my back, causing my teeth the clack over my tongue. The taste of copper fills my mouth signaling that I have definitely punctured my tongue. *Asshole.*

Without a word, or even a grunt, Ham disappears out of the room and slams the door. A click of a lock is barely audible; probably because the same too-light cream carpet covers this room, as well.

I take a moment to look around but find very little that's helpful. There are no windows, the one door we came through, and the only furniture in the room is the bed I'm lying on.

I look down around me and am barely able to turn my head enough to see that what I'm lying on has a curved Navy Blue headboard. *Wait, that's not a headboard.* I look over everything again and realize I'm on a fold-out couch of some kind.

The sheets and pillowcases are a crisp white and match the built-in bookshelves on the wall to my right. But, like the rest of the room, there isn't a single thing on them. Not a book, a pen, a speck of dust. *Lukas either has a maid or he doesn't live here. He was always a slob.*

After another ten minutes, I start to feel the prickly sensations of my body parts coming back to life. I spend at least three minutes forcing my limbs to move. It takes every ounce of energy I can muster but I'm finally able to roll over. I slowly tuck my hands between my legs and stare at the empty bookshelf. My body is screaming at me. My ribs, my stomach, my face, my everything; it all aches in ways I've never experienced before.

The events from this never-ending day press down on me and my eyes begin to close. I don't know the last time I laid on something resembling an actual mattress. So, I decide to let myself go; drifting off to sleep, knowing my nightmares will still be here when I wake up.

25

Annie

A sharp poke in my neck makes me gasp out loud. I feel the mattress lift as if someone is moving away from my back. I rush to sit up, groaning as the room spins.

Movement from my left catches my attention and I turn to face him; no, *them*. Lukas is leaning against the blank wall, arms crossed over his chest and legs crossed at his ankles. The sneer on his face and fire in his eyes lets me know I'm about to be chewed up and spit out because of my little stunt on the boat.

My limbs grow heavier but I force myself to turn, just a little more, to take in the man to Lukas' right. *Fuck. Me.*

"N-n..." I try swallowing around what feels like a rock in my throat and try again. "N-no. P-p-p-lee..."

Lukas barks out a laugh. "Oh kitten," he tsks. "I'm so glad you remember my good friend. I decided that Brute could sit this one out and, Greaser here, could pay you a visit. I mean, it has been a while."

Greaser. Figures. He does look greasy. His teeth are a grisly yellow and the harsh scent of damp tobacco hangs thick in the air. He's bald now and has a huge tattoo of a spider sitting on the right side of his head, making its way up and over to the left. His beer belly is bigger than before, but his arms look like he stuffed bowling balls through the top of his sleeves.

Nausea builds in my stomach, the acid rises up enough to tickle the back of my throat. I move to wrap my arm around my stomach but can't lift my hand. Panic settles deep in my body as I realize *what* had woken me up.

Lukas circles the mattress and my head becomes increasingly difficult to move. I can feel it slowly lolling forward but fight whatever the drugs were; trying to keep my eyes on him. He stops in front of the mattress, grinning like the maniac who haunts my dreams. "You, my fierce little bitch, have now killed *two* of my men."

I try to ask what he's talking about but can't get my mouth to move. Thankfully, my face must show my confusion. His face contorts in anger as he sucks his breath through his teeth. "I just got a fucking call from Pyro, his brother has been in a coma since you went feral on him. But, tonight, his body gave out. And tonight, you killed Kane! So you, you stupid fucking cunt, *you* have killed two of my men. *Mine!*"

He screams the last word, punctuating it by grabbing my legs and yanking me hard enough that my back slams onto the bed.

I try to kick out, try to move, but the drug has taken over. He squeezes my ankle and pain blazes up through my leg. I want to cry out, but I can't. Tears fill my eyes, shrouding my vision, as he continues his villainous monologue.

"You have always been a difficult little bitch and, based on your *behavior*, it seems like there's no reason to keep you around; you're only causing me *fucking problems*. So, I made a deal with Greaser. He gets you for a full 24 hours. Apparently he liked your disgusting pussy; although I can't imagine why." He sneers and looks at me like I'm absolute filth before continuing. "Anyways, he can act out all his little depraved fantasies then, he'll get rid of you." He flicks his wrist like he's shooing away a dirty dog on the street.

Releasing my ankle, he stands up, rolling up his sleeves before shoving his hands in his pockets. "Don't worry kitten, I'll make sure the kids have a nice life."

I can feel the tears overflowing from my eyes. His face fills with equal parts malice and promise. He clears his throat, looks over at Greaser, and nods. Without another word, he turns and quickly makes his way out the door.

My eyes find Greaser standing in the same spot, far too my left. I can't move my head and a whimper almost escapes me. I'm not sure what's worse; fighting and losing, like in the past, or not being able to fight at all.

Tears continue to flow down, soaking into my hair. Thankfully, I *can* close my eyelids, which may be super helpful for the next 24 hours.

I close my eyes and start taking deep, steadying breaths as I prepare to find the void. Rough, calloused hands begin squeezing my breasts, causing me to internally jump in fear. Then, he begins smacking each of them.

Smack
Smack
Smack
Smack

The sting spreads over, around, and through each breast. Fear heightens inside me as I fight to get to my void. Pain sears on each side of my jaw as he clamps his hand and squeezes the bone on each side. My eyes fly open and I look deep into the eyes of my death; my reaper.

Stomach acid climbs up my throat as the smell of rotting food and Goldschlager fans across my face. His eyes are black; blown wide in sadistic pleasure. "You filled out so nicely. I love this flabby belly and dented thighs. Mmmm so many places to mark you."

He inhales deeply as he drags his nose up my neck. Then he uses his tongue to draw a line from above his finger on my jaw, up my cheek, and ending in my hairline. Disgust fills me in more than fifty ways but I'm fucking trapped inside my own body.

He pinches my nipple with his other hand and yanks hard as he releases, causing my breast to stretch out before flopping down like a jelly mold. I can't take the pain or the shame anymore. And I already know what's next.

I force myself to stare into his eyes, finding the black void, and grabbing hold of it. As his face distorts and the feelings fizzle, I see the opening I need, and jump through.

I blink my eyes and immediately relax as the vast nothingness surrounds me. After a moment, a door appears. I take my time strolling to it; wanting to soak in every moment alone.

When I reach the shiny silver handle, I rest my hand on top of it for a moment, before pressing down on it and pushing the door open. It opens wide and I take in the scene before me. My attention immediately lands on my kids running around the front yard; laughing and splashing around in their inflatable water slide.

But, something is different than the other scenes I've been through. This isn't a real memory.

Realizing that, I step forward a few feet and widen my eyes as I see the guys, my Gospel Boys, laughing together with my mom. They're all so relaxed; so happy.

Vince is filling water balloons for the kids, Jenson is in a water gun fight with Josh, Cory is grilling hamburgers and hot dogs, and Nick is chilling with Reginald on his shoulder while talking with Mom about the youth center. The scene makes my heart fill with emotion. I lean against the Suburban, parked in the street, and take a moment to watch; just *needing* to soak it all up.

A loud boom rattles around us, shaking the scene like an earthquake. No one reacts; they just keep soaking up the sun, enjoying each other's company.

Another boom vibrates around me followed by what sounds like firecrackers. I look around the yard, trying to figure out if I'm combining a July 4th celebration or something but it appears I'm the only one that hears the noise.

My breath is swiftly and painfully expelled from my body and I fight to draw in another one. It feels like there's an elephant on my chest and the void begins to dull. "Noooooo! Please, no!" I try to cry out; desperate to stay here with them.

Fireworks and firecrackers burst out all around me. The loud sounds, the pressure on my chest, the screaming, the stench of smoke filling my nose; it's all overloading my system and I'm thrown into a panic attack.

My heart beats painfully against my ribs as I try to open my eyes and fail. It reminds me of the times I've been trapped in a nightmare, trying to wake up, but I'm stuck right in the middle of dream and reality.

I try to breathe. I try to see. I try, I try, I fucking try!

But, I can't. I can't. *I can't.*

I'm frozen inside my body and mind with no way to get out.

Suddenly, the pressure on my chest vanishes. I try to suck in deep breaths but my panic attack is preventing me from inhaling *and* exhaling like a normal damn person. There's more shouting, more fireworks, but none of it makes sense. My mind is a chaotic mess of images and sounds and I have no way to confirm or disprove what my overactive imagination is conjuring.

Instead of focusing on breathing, I try to focus on moving. Begging, pleading, praying that I can get one pinky to lift, one toe to twitch. But, I *can't*. It won't work.

Anxiety grips me by the throat and wraps her tentacles around me as she squeezes mercilessly. As I begin choking for air, I feel something wrap around my body.

This is it. I know it is. He must be done and he's going to just bury me or throw me in the water. I'm going to die and I'll never see my babies again.

Did I hug them when I dropped them off at Mom's? Did I tell them how special they are? How much they are loved?

I feel the faint trickle of tears running down my face as breathing continues to be difficult. I think a small whimper may have escaped my lips because I suddenly hear, "Shit. Shhhh. Shhhhh. It's ok. You're ok."

The voice startles me but I still can't get my eyelids to move. It's not a voice I can place and I know it's not *Greaser's*. But, none of the men have been nice to me since I was taken. *Why is* he? *What does he want?*

All at once my mind picks up on dozens of tiny details; details that help regulate my breathing ever so slightly.

I'm being held, cradled tightly against someone. *Not* like I'm being disposed of, but carefully carried. *When did he pick me up? Oh, maybe when I was wrapped up.*

Wait, wrapped up... With each jostle of movement, I can feel the semi-soft material around my body. I can feel it around my shoulders and all the way down to my feet. No breeze blows through; except my hair. *My head isn't covered.* It's supported; like in the crook of someone's arm. *And, he's trying to comfort me.*

My breathing calms a little more, sort of, and I try my damndest to focus on what I can hear. My body is slightly bumping up and down with each step. There's still fireworks and yelling. All men; all screaming. The heavy thud of pounding feet can be heard over the shattering of glass.

Suddenly, my body is jostled and my back slams into a wall and, I think, the guy's arm that's wrapped around my back. I hear the man grunt out a "fuck" before regaining balance and moving faster.

In a matter of moments, we're bumping down what must be the rest of the stairs, then crunching across something. It sounds like rubble and debris. Before I can process any more, a biting wind whips my hair across my shoulders. I try to snuggle deeper into the man while my body jostles harder but, again, I can't. With the way my body is jumping and his breaths are growing heavier, I think he's now running. *Dude must be ripped to run with me in his arms.*

I focus on his labored breaths to try and match them since I'm still just a notch below hyperventilating. The cold bites into my cheeks and lashes at my feet; now sticking out from under the sheet. We come to an abrupt stop before I feel his knee raise up and kick out. It sounds like he's kicking a door of some kind. "It's M. Open up. I got the one Lukas brought back."

The sound of a van door rolling open echoes out and I realize that the fireworks seem much further away. I'm handed off to someone else who cradles me against his chest right before he slams himself back against a wall with a grunt, "Hold on Siren, I've got you. Oh my God! I've got you."

Why does it sound like he's going to cry? Why does that voice sound so familiar? Has my line between fantasy and reality really blurred so much that I'm hearing them outside of dissociation?

The space fills with chatter, pulling me from my thoughts. I hear a deep voice snap out, "Boss" then he rattles off things before banging something twice and shouting, "Team 1 has to roll out. Number 4 is still inside. The rest of you stay. Team three is on their way to restore the lights. Meet at the rockets when done." A loud beep rings out as the van door slams shut; spiking my anxiety.

Oh my God, they're taking me somewhere else. I can't survive anything else. I can't. I don't want to go back to the dungeon. I try to move, try to scream, try to open my eyes but I can't. My heart is beating so rapidly that I'm positive I'm going to have a heart attack. A whimper barely escapes through my lips and the arms around me tighten.

Smooth skin glides down my cheek as the man who's holding me leans over my head that is still secured against his chest. He starts whispering but it's a jumble of words that doesn't make sense over the whooshing in my ears. He continues whispering and I feel him slowly start rocking me side-to-side as the van picks up speed.

Eventually, my heart begins to slow and the man's words seep into my ears; forcing themselves into my brain. "It's ok, Siren. I've got you. We got you. We've got you, Siren. We're never letting you go. Never, Annie, I swear. Oh, God, Annie, I swear."

My heart stutters in my chest as his words penetrate the fog in my brain. A choked out sob breaks free from my throat as tears leak from my eyes; again. *He's here. But how?*

I still can't talk, still can't move, but I feel like I can start to breathe. *Finally.*

I let his gentle words wash over me as I breathe deeper, steadier, and work on lowering my heart rate. I inhale deeply and his perfect scent fills me with relief. *Summer rain and lavender. My Nick. He's here. He's actually here.*

And that's the last thought I have before fatigue pulls me under.

26

Vince- Thirty Minutes Ago

Nick and I pile into the same van and he immediately brings his laptop to life, clicking on buttons at lightning speed. I watch as the screen fills with tiny videos from cameras he's been able to hack into.

Nick taps his ear piece before saying, "Team 1: check." Then the rest of the teams check-in. After all 6 teams give the green light, we pull out.

Enzo's voice filters through the comms, "Message from my guy. Something happened and they had to come back. Only some of the merchandise was moved."

Nick begins rewinding the footage around the house. After a moment, Nick clicks his ear piece, "Confirmed. Group Alpha, I've confirmed five men going back. They unloaded eleven girls."

Jenson's voice rings out, "Alpha team copy. Five known targets."

Nick clicks his ear piece, again, "Team Bravo: seventeen men total at the house. One took a girl in the house after everyone else unloaded. Too dark to see her but there's at least one innocent."

Rocco's voice confirms in my ear before Nick speaks, again. "Team Bravo: 3 armed in the backyard, right against the house, 1 armed on the boat, 2 on each side of the house and 2 at the front door. Remaining 7, including Lukas, in the house."

Mateo confirms and the van fills with silence except for the fast clicking of Nick pounding the keys on the keyboard.

I try not to ask. I do. But, I can't help it, "Is it her, Nick?"

He shakes his head before looking at me with steely eyes, "I can't tell. It doesn't matter how much I zoom in, it's too dark at the back of the house." I give him my best reassuring smile before nodding. I need to refocus on the mission so I turn and face the front window, watching the dark road stretch out in front of us.

I spend the next few minutes mentally preparing myself. This is the same as any other takedown I've been part of. *Only, we plan on killing every asshole we find. And this is super illegal. And we had to use Enzo's connections to make sure none of this could be traced back to us.*

But, yeah, same-same.

I breathe in through my nose deeply and push it out of my mouth; expelling any negativity, any fear, any doubt. Even if Annie isn't here, even if they offloaded her, the Italians up north will get her. I know they will. And, at the end of the day, I'll have satisfaction in knowing this asshat and all his shitty friends will no longer be a problem for me, for Annie, and for any poor woman that has ever had the displeasure of meeting them.

I idly run my thumb over my holster, allowing the cool leather to ground me. I'm so ready for this to be over.

We make our way through the small, bay-side community to the mouth of the cul-de-sac that the house sits on. The electric company van, the one I'm in, pulls up to the light pole that is closest to the house; maybe sixty feet away. The water company van parks further up the street on the opposite side, near a sewage drain.

I noticed a couple of other vehicles following us through the neighborhood. One stopped near the street opening and another one parks on the street, two houses away from our target. Nick points out that they're all with us so I settle a little more. I didn't even hear the command for them to follow.

Rocco's voice filters through the comms, "Alright guys. Clean up crew is already stationed and have stripped six wires around the house." We nod in understanding. *Awesome six less guys in our way and no one was alerted of their demise.*

Nick pipes in, "Bravo; 7 confirmed in the house. 3 in the backyard, 1 at the boat."

"Copy" rang over the comms before Mateo chimes in. "Get ready to blow and go boys."

I smirk, knowing what he's about to do. Just before the boom rattles through the air, I tug Nick in by the neck, firmly planting my lips to his. I keep it short but pour all I have into it. When I release him, he gives me a warm smile and mouths "love you" before I hop out of the van and run like my ass is on fire.

I follow behind three other guys in tac gear; feeling more coming up behind me. The crunch of the debris from the door can barely be heard over the sound of shouting and gun fire, but I'm trained for this. I narrow down all of my senses until I can pinpoint each threat.

A couple men gathered in the living room, using the couch and overturned dining table for cover. A tap on my left shoulder alerts me that one of our guys is headed up the stairs we stopped near and I nod my agreement; not taking my eyes off the room in front of me.

Smoke fills the air and one of the pricks raises his gun just above the couch and starts blindly shooting. "Fucker" I grit through my teeth as a bullet grazes my arm just as I roll to the side, using the far left hallway for coverage. I peek out and see that there is just enough of a gap under the couch to see movement. My grin turns feral as I move to execute. Army crawling across the floor, I make my way into the living room. *Amateurs.*

I look behind me and see one guy in the right hallway who nods at me, and another who's made his way into the kitchen. A few gunshots ring out from behind me, up the stairs. I turn my head as another man whistles for my attention. He holds up one hand and signs e-n-z-o with the other. It only takes me half a second to remember this must be the guy Enzo had on the inside. I nod at him and watch as he sprints from the hallway, clears the foyer and maneuvers up the stairs like he's fucking Spider-Man.

I turn back just as a spray of bullets goes off above my head and watch as debris from the walls and staircase fly into the air. Just when I see two sets of knees hit the floor, I pick them off, one-by-one. Their shock and pain gives my guy in the kitchen long enough to run out to the back; the guy in the hall hot on his heels.

I jump up, keeping my head down and gun trained in front of me, and maneuver around the left side of the table. I crouch right at the side of the couch as the staccato of gunfire from the backyard fills the air. Windows shatter and screams fill the night.

I peer around the couch and see one asshole has abandoned his gun completely; grabbing on to both knees, rocking on his back, and screaming out in agony. The other is gasping while leaning his head against the couch, but his gun is still in his hand.

Not wanting to catch a bullet to the face, I roll to the back side of the couch and tuck into a tight squat. I listen to their sounds, tracking any movement, before counting back from three. At 'one', I quickly pop up, and fire downwards, nailing the roly poly bastard in the head.

Before I can squat back down, the other guy shoots up, and uses his arms to fling himself almost completely over the couch, shooting wildly. One of the bullets barely misses me but I hear someone behind me grunt. *Must be one of the guys from the stairs.*

Froggie's body is half hanging over the back of the couch, as he struggles with pain in of his movements. I whip my hand out and slam it down on his, causing him to fire a shot into the floor. Then, I grab the wrist holding the gun, turn my body facing the stairs and drag him forward; knowing his knees are rubbing painfully against the top of the couch. When I feel a little resistance, I twist the gun in his hand, keeping my left hand on his right one, and shoot a hole straight through his face.

His body sags over the couch and I exhale heavily. Then, I pick up my gun and wobble towards the back. By the time I enter the kitchen, I hear someone on the comms, "Team 1 has to roll out. Number 4 is still inside. The rest of you stay. Team three is on their way to restore the lights. Meet at the rockets when done."

I shakily reach up to click the ear piece. "Number 4 copy. Check-in Team Bravo."

Within seconds, every one of the men checks in; only two need assistance. "All wires fixed?" I wait, holding my breath, as each person answers through the comms with a "check".

I blow out a painful breath, clenching my teeth as the past few minutes crash down on me. I know we aren't done but it feels so, freeing, knowing it really happened. And *we* helped.

Mateo's voice crackles on the comms, "ID sweep then set-up for departure." Nodding to myself, I wobble back over to the asshats lying in the living room. I check all of their pockets but come up empty. I can get facial recognition from one since I only clipped the side of his head, but, uh, definitely not the other. I snap a quick picture before turning back to the stairs, remembering one of the men who needs assistance is upstairs.

I take two at a time, trying to get to him quickly, and knowing we need to evacuate. The guy, Lars, I think, is gasping for breath.

His eyes are glossy and you can see thick red lines that mark his neck. Someone had clearly tried to strangle him. *Presumably the ugly asshole lying dead behind him with a gunshot wound to the face.*

He lifts a shaky hand, pointing into the room. His voice comes out hoarse, no doubt from the pressure that was put on his throat. "Make sure that fuckwad is dead. He was on top of the girl but I had a struggle right after I shot him. I never made it in. M grabbed her, though." His breathing is labored, and I know he needs medical attention, but I'm glad he's making sure we check everyone.

I make quick work of tearing off part of my shirt to use as a makeshift bandage. I wrap it around the bullet wound in his leg to slow the bleeding, tying it off tight and causing him to hiss in pain. Once it's secure, I hit the earpiece as I step in the room, "Need another box up here. System is leaking and damaged."

I didn't even hear anyone comment as I take in the room around me. The flabby bastard with giant arms is lying face down on the carpet. His shirt is off and his pants are half way around his ankles. Bile builds in my throat as my mind paints a picture of what the man was doing before Lars intervened. I shake my head to clear the horrendous images and roll him over with my boot. "Hey 4," One of the other guys pops his head in. "We're taking 7. Sixty seconds."

I study the bastard's face for all of five seconds before deciding to not to even check for a pulse. I don't know if he got what he was trying to but, I don't care. After snapping a picture of his face, I empty the entire clip of my second gun in his face. Turning, I jog down the stairs and run out of the house, thankful that the last van is open and waiting for me.

I dive in and slam the door shut. Matteo's voice rings out, "Bravo check for departure." Everyone was already in their vehicles and ready to go. Just as we turn off the street, multiple blasts ricochet through the air. I watch in grim fascination as Lukas' whole fucking world explodes; literally.

Smirking to myself, I turn towards the windshield and watch as we make our way through the coastal community; back to the rendezvous point.

Once we arrive, we pile out and swiftly walk into the large open warehouse. I scan the area but don't see any of my guys. Fear grows in my belly and takes root in my soul. *I was in the last vehicle to arrive. Everyone should already be here.*

Enzo whistles for everyone to quiet down and we all loosely gather around him, Rocco, and Mateo. The big metal doors are rolled shut and locked in place. The inside looks more like an airport hangar than a warehouse. It only has a few industrial lights around the area and the ceiling is so tall that his voice echoes off the ceilings. "Beautiful job boys. Today, twelve women were rescued. They're all at the hospital and we will help them, quietly, in any way we can. As you know, we made plenty of precautions making sure not a single one of us can be tied to this evening's *festivities*."

His smirk shows just how much he enjoyed handing Lukas his ass. His eyes shimmer with pride and respect as he looks at each of us. "At this time, we have six in the medical unit and none of their injuries appear to be life threatening. We'll get more updates later. We had no fatalities. So, thank you. I appreciate every one of you."

Enzo beams a smile at Rocco, who steps forward, "Now, you all have your individual assignments for how to leave here and your plans for the next few days; until we say otherwise. If you have any questions, let us know, if not, fuck off and enjoy the rest of the week." He grins and chuckles to himself and some of the others join in.

Once a path becomes clear, I stride up to them and stick my hand out to shake his. "Thank you so much Enzo. You have no idea how much I appreciate this."

His smile crinkles his eyes as he returns my handshake, "Of course. I'm happy to help." He looks over me in concern before asking if I need medical attention, too. I shake my head and let him know it's just a graze.

"So, do you know where my guys are?" Enzo quickly nods, "Yes. Cory needed attention and Jenson went with him. We can take you there now."

He looks toward Mateo and smiles so wide it's almost unnerving. "Nick is getting cleaned up at a hotel. It's just around the corner from the hospital that the women were taken to. It was a struggle, but we finally convinced him to let her go."

Her? Let who go? Confusion must have been evident on my face as Rocco steps forward, grasps my shoulder in a friendly squeeze and meets my eyes. "Mikas grabbed her from the house. He got her out, Vince. She's safe."

Images assault my brain like multiple movies being played at the same time. I feel myself drop to the floor as my vision blurs. Hands squeeze my shoulders and pat my back as I sob out my fear, my pain, my worry, my relief. And they let me. *Scary criminals my ass.*

My sobs turn into laughter before I finally accept help to pull myself from the ground. I look at each of them while wiping my face. "Holy shit. Ok. Ok, what now?"

Enzo shoves his hands into his pockets, smiles wide, and tilts his head and looks at me. "Whatever you want."

I can feel the smile stretching across my face and relish in the knowledge that my family will be whole again soon.

27

Nick

Holy crackerballs! She's here. Well, not here-here but, not there. Being forced to hand her over to one of Enzo's men so they could cover our tracks at the hospital was the hardest thing I have ever had to do.

She's safe; finally safe. She was breathing; but not moving. Which scares the shit out of me. I could tell when she finally realized it was me in the van. Her body began to relax and my heart almost imploded. I didn't know what else to say or do so I held on with every fiber of my being and kept repeating what I hoped were comforting words.

I've been at the hotel that Enzo set up for the guys and I for about fifteen minutes. I was supposed to shower and wait for them. Our bags were already delivered here, which is great, I think. I'm just too fucking wound up. I'm pacing back and forth, listening to the whir of the A/C unit by the window.

I look towards the door, again, hoping someone will step through. *Fuck, where are they?* Suddenly, I stop my pacing, mid-step. "Oh, duh Nick. Trackers." I ran over to my bag and pulled out my phone, unlocking the screen and clicking on the app. Enzo has all of our trackers but we only have access to each other.

We had to leave our phones in our bags during the mission but we all got trackers inserted in the underside of our arms. At first, Cory refused. We explained that if anything ever happened, Enzo had given me the program, too, so I could track us anywhere. It took him a minute but the reality of the situation we were running into finally settled him. He caved shortly after that.

Clicking on the app's map, I see Cory and Jense are near each other. Judging by the map it looks like they're at the medic warehouse. *Oh fuck! Are they ok? Dingle damn. I don't even have a car.*

Just as my brain begins spiraling into oblivion, the sound of the card reader on the door beeps. I hear the snick of the handle turning as I retrieve the gun still in the back of my pants. The latch catches the door from opening fully.

"Wrong room, Asshole," was all I could say without giving into the tremble working its way through my body.

A rich, warm chuckle sounds through the crack of the door before I see Vince's big, strong hand slide through; showing off the lava stone bracelet we bought together last year. "Asshole, huh? I don't know. I kind of think this might be the right room."

It takes me a full minute before my brain processes, then I'm running towards the door. "Hold on."

He slips his hand back out and I close the door quickly, flip the metal latch, then re-open the door. I don't even give him a second before abruptly flinging myself into his arms. The scent of gun smoke and sweat with an undercurrent of Sandalwood fills my nose as I bury my face in his neck. A sob breaks loose from my throat and he begins backing me into the room.

I feel one of his arms move, closing the door, and flipping the lock before embracing me again. We stand there, chests heaving, tears flowing, and just hold each other.

I don't know how much time passes but we've both settled enough to at least step back and take each other in. I see the torn fabric of his sleeve and immediately start ripping his shirt open, stripping off the kevlar, and zeroing in on the wound on his arm.

"Jesus, Vince. Why didn't you go to the medic building?" I push him into the bathroom and turn the water to hot.

"It's just a graze, Pretty Boy, it's fine." I huff as I run back out of the bathroom and tear into my duffle, retrieving the first aid kit I always keep in there. I start rummaging through it as I walk back to him, setting out the glue, gauze, bandages, and antibiotic cream.

I run a washcloth under the water and begin cleaning his arm. He sits quietly and lets me work but I can feel his eyes boring into the side of my face.

As the dried blood, and some of the new blood is cleared, I get more agitated with his assessment. "Dammit Vince. This needs real stitches! I can stick my whole damn pinky in this divot!"

He huffs out a sigh but doesn't comment. I tip the bottle of alcohol over the wound and ignore the hiss he releases. Taking the suture kit from the box, I start sanitizing the needle. I reach behind him to grab a hand towel and hand it to him, "Bite down, big boy."

Thankfully, he doesn't argue, although the tilt of his lip and quirk of his brow tells me he definitely wants to. The moment the towel is in his mouth, I start stitching him up; or at least, trying to. This wound is fucking deep and definitely needs a real doctor to look at it. The repetitive movement soothes me and opens my mind to thoughts of Annie again. *Did she start moving? Is she ok? How long will we have to wait to see her?*

After a few minutes, staying lost in my head, I tie off the end, snip the string, and start bandaging it. Vince removes the cloth from his mouth before speaking. "I haven't heard from the others, yet. Enzo says we had no losses on our side but Cory and Jense are at the medic building." I nod my head, having already seen this information on the phone.

After washing my hands, I quietly begin packing up the remaining supplies. "Nick, look at me. Talk to me, please."

The pain in his voice causes me to snap out of my own head. When my eyes meet his, I see all the emotions, all the questions, all the fear. "I-I held her. Vince, I *held* her. I had her in my arms and they made me give her over to the hospital and come back *here* to wait. Just *wait*. Wait for what?! We should be there. We should..." My blubbering is cut off by the sob that wrenches itself free. Vince immediately has me wrapped in his arms as he slides to the ground. He holds me close, shushing me quietly, while rocking me in his arms.

As our tears subside, exhaustion from this insane day gives way and we both fall into a fitful sleep, right there, on the bathroom floor.

28

Cory

The images replay in my mind on an infinite loop. The playback in my mind like a fucking horror movie stuck on repeat.

Jenson's smile when Enzo's voice tells us to wait for the signal.
The blast from the grenade spraying out smoke and chunks of the brick wall.
Following Jense through the destroyed opening, squinting through the smoke and debris.
Jenson turning towards the left wall while I take the right.
A dark image jumping through the smoke.

The spark from me shooting the gun.
Blood splattering my eyes and hair.
Seeing someone else run away through the smoke.
The smoke clearing enough to watch him throw open a metal door.
Following him down concrete stairs to a fucking dungeon within the dungeon.
Being ambushed by him and another fucker.
No walls to hide behind; just cells marred with blood and whatever else.
A punch flying at my face.
The ground rising up to meet me.
Boots coming down.
Sparks flying from my gun repeatedly until the chamber clicks empty.
Darkness.
Then the dark, dank ceiling.
Crawling across the bodies and stabbing them in the heart, just in case.
Pulling myself up using the rusted cell bars.
Sliding my hand across the bars, shuffling across the sticky floor, checking all the cells.
Cells with chains, hooks, drains.
Darkness when I close my eyes to blot out the possibilities.

I don't remember turning back around or making it back up the short set of stairs. I barely remember seeing Jenson on the opposite side of the room before collapsing.

At some point, I must have passed out because when my eyes open, I find myself looking at steel beams crossing the top of the high ceiling. Bright lights burn through my eyes. A bag of fluid is attached to a tube, connecting to a needle impaled in my arm. White curtains are pulled around a bar like a make-shift hospital room.

I don't know how much time passes as I replay the events from the day. I violently *killed* people today. I killed *three* people. They were vile bastards but *I killed* them. Watched as the lights extinguished from their eyes. And, honestly, I can't figure out how I feel about it. I'm disgusted with myself, sure, but they deserved it. *Right? Does that make it better? Knowing the world is better off?*

As I begin second-guessing myself, a face comes into view. Unkempt, dirty brown hair falls out of his man-bun. Emerald green eyes shine with worry, fear, exhaustion, and hope as they peer into mine; piercing through my heart.

"Cory?" My name sounds more like a plea from his lips. His eyes fill with unshed tears and his lips tremble violently.

"Cor? Cor, can you hear me?" I lick my dry lips and he quickly disappears out of view. Just as I inhale a shaky breath, he returns and places a straw between my lips. "Small sips, Cor. Good. That's good."

When I lean back away from the straw, I try again, "J-Jens-son. Are y-you ok?"

Tears fall from his lashes as he huffs out a laugh, smiling wide and shaking his head. "Yeah. I'm good. And you will be, too. Doc says you have a concussion and gash on your head that needed five stitches. You're also looking like quite the badass with a wicked black eye, split lip, and a couple of broken ribs. No internal damage but you have to rest for a couple of weeks."

I focus on processing his words for so long that I flinch when he moves to hold my hand. Once I look down at the place we're joined, my smile lifts and I squeeze his hand in return.

"The others?" My words barely slip out but I can tell he hears me. Jenson's smile widens, covering his entire face and causing his eyes to crinkle in the corners.

"Nick is at the hotel getting cleaned up. Vince went to meet him." He licks his lips and looks around for a moment. Now that his head is turned, I notice tears falling from his eyes. I can feel my eyebrows pinch in confusion because the tears don't match the smile.

He returns his gaze to mine and the emotion in his eyes causes my breath to stutter in my chest. "They got her, man. Someone got her to Nick and they took her straight to the hospital. They got her, Cor!" His voice breaks off into a sob and I find myself joining in the emotional release.

I grasp Jenson's hand tighter as we fall apart together; willing myself to get stronger, be stronger, for her. She's home, she's free, but she'll need all the help she can get to overcome this new trauma. And I'll be damned if I'm not there to see her through it.

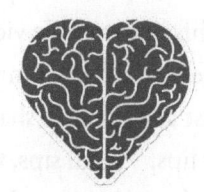

I must have fallen asleep because the next thing I hear is the deep timbre of Vince's voice and an unfamiliar male. My head is pounding and my stomach is screaming but I miss the comfort of the darkness I was in.

"I know you're awake Cor." Jense whispers in my ear. My hairs stand up on the back of my neck and I feel my cock harden. *Fuck. No! Now is definitely not the time. Those feelings need to stay buried.*

Thankfully, my dick deflates the moment I hear someone start talking about the other women they dropped off. I only hear the tail end of it, but it gives me some relief that they're all safe.

I gently open my eyes to find Jenson to my left, leaning towards me in his chair but his head is turned towards Vince. He's standing at the end of my bed with another man. One of Enzo's, I guess.

Vince comments, "That's fucking awesome. What a relief. I haven't heard from my Captain, yet, but it sounds like everything went exactly as planned. This was absolutely the best-case scenario. Minus the injuries."

I go to take a deep breath and reposition myself but end up hissing through my teeth before groaning in pain. Vince whips his head to me before smiling wide. "Good to see you, man. Need some more meds? Jense said doc can administer the next set if you need more."

I'm already shaking my head trying to clear it from the fog. "No" I croak out, my throat still dry and hoarse. I try to swallow but it feels like I licked a sand dune's butt-crack.

Jenson's already leaning a cup towards my mouth and I drink greedily, relishing how it soothes my entire mouth and throat. I slowly sit all the way up, failing at covering my grunt of pain. Sweat beads my forehead as I try again, "No hard meds. Just give me Tylenol and let's go. I want to see Annie."

Vince's brows furrow and his lips tighten in a frown. "We can't."

I snap my eyes to his, anger boiling in my veins. Before I can spew my thoughts, his hands come up in a placating gesture, his brows and eyes softening. "Cory. We can't go, yet. We have to wait until we're notified. We aren't even supposed to know she's free, remember?"

I go to cut him off but he continues, "Enzo has people all over that damn hospital and they'll be there until all of the women are released to go home. But, until then, we *have* to wait. You *know* we do."

My heart beats erratically as I try to come up with some way to see her for myself. To know she really is ok. I know the plan, and I logically understand why, but I hate the thought of her waking up without us. I can't take it.

Vince must sense my resolve slipping as he crosses to the right side of the bed before laying his hand on my shoulder and gently squeezing. "I know, man. I know. But she is safe. We can't be there for her if what we did is found out. For now, we just need to rest and recharge. With any luck, her mom will be notified soon and maybe she'll call us later. So, let's go back to the room, eat, rehydrate, and get some rest because, once I'm in that room, I'm not letting her out of my sight."

His whispered words help to calm the roar of my heart and shift my brain back into being in control. His steely resolve helps to rebuild mine as I stare into his eyes. The sincerity and ferocity in his statement forces me to take a deep breath and acquiesce. I know. *I know this is best. I know she's safe. And I know we'll see her soon.*

I repeat those thoughts as my heart rate slows and my eyelids slowly drift shut again.

29

Annie

Nope, fuck this... and I jumped back into the welcoming arms of darkness.

A note from the author

Oh my stars! Are you ok? Do you need anything? Have you had any water? How about a scream session?

Seriously, though. Thank you for staying on this journey with Annie and her men. I really thought we'd get some spice in this one but, the book decided to take it's own direction.

While I am sorry that I have left you with a "Happy-ish For Now", I solemnly swear that book three is coming right up.

Annie and her men have a lot of healing to do, and maybe a hurtle, or five, to jump but an HEA is on the horizon.

Thank you, thank you, thank you for being part of this story with me. I look forward to diving into more stories in the future but it wouldn't be worth it without you!

If you liked, or loved, this book, please remember to leave a review and let me know!

Want updates, sneak-peaks, and to see the inner-workings of my scary mind?

Join the Tris Wynters' Warriors on Facebook https://www.facebook.com/groups/1422660571980693/
Follow me on TiktTok @TrisWynterswrites

Acknowledgements

A big thank you to my husband, Jeff, who spent countless hours talking with me about boats, houses, and waterways. Seriously, it was a chore and he patiently walked me through what could be possible and how the characters could execute certain parts of my plan.

Of course, a huge thank you to my Bestest Ohana bitch, Kayla. Not only is she my editor and best friend but she is so good at talking me out of my head when I over-edit.

Last, but never least, thank you to those of you who have read this book. I know this one had a lot of emotions and promise healing is coming.

I adore you all and can't express my gratitude enough.

Milton Keynes UK
Ingram Content Group UK Ltd.
UKHW042032070324
439097UK00001B/1

9 798989 804528